I0717826

Betrayed

Am I My Sister's Keeper?

Anitra Ferguson

Betrayed

Copyright © 2019 by Anitra Ferguson.

All rights reserved. No part of this book may be reproduced or transmitted in any form or by any means, electronic or mechanical, including photocopying, recording, or by any information storage and retrieval system, without permission in writing from the copyright owner.

This is a work of fiction. Names, characters, places and incidents either are the product of the author's imagination or are used fictitiously, and any resemblance to any actual persons, living or dead, events, or locales is entirely coincidental.

ISBN: 978-1-970135-32-9 paperback
978-1-970135-33-6 ebook

Published in the United States by Pen2Pad Ink Publishing.

Requests to publish work from this book or to contact the author should be sent to: anitrawrites2018@gmail.com

Anitra Ferguson retains the rights to all images.

Betrayed

"Ohhhhh! Yessss, baby, yesss, babyy! Oh shit, this feels so damn good!" Sand was saying while smiling with eyes closed. *Pop pop pop pop.* Four shots sounded off in the small room seemingly from nowhere.

"Ohh fuck, Murder! Why you do dat?" Earlene screamed. "Ohhh my god, ohhh my god!" She screamed again while simultaneously running around in circles then falling to her knees, scared out of her mind. "Shut the fuck up, bitch, and get the fuck up off your knees. Help me get rid of this motherfucker's body! Listen and learn; never think you can get away with fucking over Murderville, 'cause I don't play that shit and I run this fucking city! Money talks and bullshit walks. If the dollar amount is right, a motherfucker will sell they soul to the highest bidder and I'd pay rather well. I am the man, Murda v-i-double-l-e!" Murder was saying all this while rolling Sand White's dead ass up in a tarp to be thrown in the river.

Mikeela "Kee-Kee" Rye

I rolled my eyes as I prepared to leave De'Lamars. This was a popular restaurant on the south side of Millville, Illinois. I had just been involved in another unsuccessful, boring-ass date with a no class having mothersucker. (I am trying to quit cussing.) "Damn, damn, damn!" I just screamed in a crowded restaurant. I didn't care about the stares I was receiving. I was totally frustrated right now. I thought that he might have been the one so I could end this single-person shit. Nine months ago, I had decided to become celibate to accommodate this new life role I had chosen to lead. You see, I rededicated my life to Christ and I wanted to lead some type of peaceful, faithful life. However, this celibate thing was turning out to be harder than I thought.

At this particular moment, *sex* was on my brain and my body had begun to betray me and demand the attention of a man. Ughh! Life can be tricky sometimes, especially when you are trying to live right. Temptations seem to always show up and show out in your weakest moments. At this particular moment, I was weak and I wanted to be sexed. I had come on this date with this man, Daniel Davis. Now he was sexy as hell, so I hadn't checked out much else about him besides his body and how he filled out a suit. His penis print was appeasing to the eyes too. Well, hell, to mine anyway! All of a sudden, I look up and both my mistake and my current situation had found me in this damn restaurant. Not only had I not made a love connection or even a lust connection, for that matter with this brother, but this loser had also left the damn place, leaving my ass to pay the check. Now ain't that about nothing?

"Ma'am, ma'am, how will you be paying for this?" The waiter asked rudely interrupting me from the conversation I was having with myself in my head.

"Umm, how much is the bill?" I asked with as much ghetto attitude and irritation I could muster up.

He handed me the bill and sashayed off. I chuckled because I needed to find the humor in something. Afterall, there certainly wasn't any in this bill or this waste of a night. What kind of man walks out on a bill and on a date that he asked me out on? I was getting pissed, so it was best that I just paid the motherfucker and took my embarrassed ass home.

The waiter came back with all these brave ass questions. "What happened to that sexy ass gentleman you was with?" I couldn't believe he had the nerve to ask me that. I just looked at him.

"Company must not have been pleasant," he continued with a slight laugh. "Better luck next time, sweetie."

"That is none of your concern! Can I get my damn receipt before I slap your sweet ass to sleep?" I said loud enough to cause another scene. I knew the people in this damn restaurant were shaking their heads at me and my antics, but I didn't care. I had a good mind to complain on the waiter, but instead, I left a big tip and a dirty note on the receipt. Kill 'em with kindness (well, kind of). You would think that with me being a successful defense attorney, with my own house and my own financial means of supporting myself, I would be able to find someone on my level to build a life with. Did I mention that I was beautiful in the face and thick in the waist, if I can toot my own horn? *Toot, toot!* Well, tomorrow is a new day, so I will shake this experience off and keep it moving.

"Ms. Rye, you have calls waiting on lines 1 and 2," Danita Wallace, my secretary, said through the intercom.

"Thank you, Mrs. Wallace," I replied, and I pressed line 1. "Hello, this is Ms. Rye. How can I be of service to you?"

"Hey, sexy, this is Daniel. I really enjoyed you last night and was wondering if we could do a second?"

"Hell naww! And where the hell is my money for your part of the dinner that you stuffed your mouth with?"

I screamed into the phone, interrupting Daniel and his lies. I was politely met with silence and then the damn dial tone in my ear.

The nerve of this motherfucker! Then he hung up in my damn face! I promise I bet not see him in the streets. It most definitely will be a misunderstanding!

"Mrs. Wallace, from now on block all calls from Mr. Daniel McNothing Davis. He has been deleted and dismissed. I also need for you to forward the rest of my personal calls for today — business only for the rest of the day."

"Yes, ma'am," Danita replied. "Your wish is my command."

I really didn't know if this bitch was trying to be funny, but I'ma let her make it today cause I had work I needed to focus on. I have dealt with all the bullshit I was going to deal with today. I had to make my coins, so for the rest of the day, I'll be focusing on my clients and their needs. Yes honey, attorney extraordinaire in full effect.

I was finally home after a long day and couldn't do anything but sigh long and hard as I made my way to the kitchen to pour me a glass of Merlot. I needed to relax after the past two days — hell, after the week I was having. I was beginning to think that I needed to take the day off, maybe even a month or a year, for that matter, to get my personal affairs in order.

The time off would allow me to refocus and

determine what I really desired from the relationships that I wanted in my life. Some decisions needed to be made because to remain single was not the life I planned on living, and it was certainly not the life I thought I would be living at this stage of my life. Maybe I was going through a midlife crisis at thirty-five years of age. However, I knew that before taking an extended vacation, I would have to think long and hard. Although I could afford to do so, I had the livelihood of my employees and clients to consider. As a successful defense attorney in Millville, I had built a nice reputation for myself, and I intend to keep it that way. So before I made a final decision, I would have to consider all my options. Law was my life and my first love, so being able to walk away for any time period would be difficult.

Damn, this wine must be good as hell if it got me thinking about vacations and shit. I gotta get another bottle as soon as possible.

I walked over to the radio in my bedroom, hit the on button, and then made my way to my spacious master bath. I could hear Charlie Wilson singing his heart out: *"There goes my baby, there goes my destiny."* I was snapping my fingers and dancing from side to side. That was my jam. I had to go back to the radio and turn it up as loud as it could go. The Merlot and Charlie had me feeling some kind of way. I danced from the radio all the way back to the bathroom and turned on the hot water and added my bubble bath, all the while still dancing and sipping on my glass of wine. I removed my robe and slid all so beautifully into the tub. I was thinking that having a man to go and cuddle with would make this night all better. Soon I hoped that my prayers would be answered. As of the present time, I was certainly in a more relaxed state and a better headspace than earlier today, so I was glad for that. I knew that at least tonight I would sleep good.

I had decided to let not having a man rest for at least tonight and removed the thought from my mind. Instead, I focused on my bath, my glass of wine, and the songs blasting from my radio.

In God's time, not Mikeela's, what is supposed to be will be.

Chanel "Co-Co" Rene Rye

"Y'all betta get somewhere and sit yo ass down and stop running in this damn house!" I screamed at my two boys. They were working my nerves this morning, and it was too damn early. I have two boys, Juju, aged four, and Lil Ray-Ray, aged three. I was trying to sleep in to at least ten o'clock, but these children of mine were loud as hell and was ignoring my ass like I wasn't screaming at the top of my lungs for them to get someplace and sit their ass down.

Damn, I knew I might as well get out of bed, but I was so tired and couldn't move. So, I rolled over and tried to return to some type of deep sleep. I was the single mother of two young children by two different men, living in the projects and stripping at one of the clubs in town. I knew my story seemed cliché, but it is what it is. I needed to provide for me and my children, and since I hadn't listened to my mother or grandmother, stripping was what I could do without much education. The street life had taken me in with open arms when I was in my teenage years. I was hotheaded, hard headed, and a fast-ass little girl who thought my shit didn't stink and that I knew every damn thing. Sooner rather than later, I found out that in fact, I didn't know shit, but by then I was in the game and it was too late to turn back. My mother was a crackhead and a hoe. She taught me to use my body and my looks to get what I wanted from men, and so that was what I did. It was funny how I decided to listen to my mother about being a hoe, but didn't listen when she was preaching about education and school. Juju knocked on my door while screaming, "Co-Co, get up! I'm hungry! I want to eat!"

I sat up on the bed and picked up my shoe and threw it at the door. It hit the door with a loud thud. "Get away from my door! I am sleeping! Uggh!" I screamed. These damn kids would not let me sleep, so reluctantly I climbed out of bed and retreated to the bathroom to wash my face and brush my teeth. For some reason, I was always thinking about my shitty-ass childhood. I had experienced a bunch of hard times. My mother, the great Earlene Rye, was a recovering crack addict. I really didn't know if she was clean or not 'cause every time you talk with a crackhead, they always talk about them being clean or going to rehab on Monday. So shit, I really didn't know her deal, and to be honest, I didn't care.

I had this love-hate relationship with my family, but especially with my mother. I just didn't trust myself to love her because I always ended up hurt and in my feelings. As a result of my childhood, I had major self-esteem issues and a great distrust of men. In my mind I believed that my body was my greatest asset, and since the tender age of six, I had been using it to my advantage to get what I needed to make it from day to day. I knew that I was a beautiful chocolate-brown woman (at least that was what men said) with hazel eyes, big luscious lips, and wide hips. My measurements are 38-24-36, if you want to know.

Curiosity killed the cat, and mine most definitely had these dudes in their shit, leaving relationships and spending *mucho dinero*; yet I remained in the projects. So was I really winning? Men most certainly went crazy when they saw me, and I took full advantage of my attributes in my current profession every night. I needed to make it rain 'cause I had bills to pay and mouths to feed. I was not the main attraction at Club Body, but I held my own and got my coins every night I was on stage, you can believe that.

Once upon a time, I had dreams that expanded outside the projects, but I was my mother's child and reality seemed to fuck that up real quick and in a hurry. I wondered if I had time to make a change. My grandmother Hattie Maye Allen used to say that God has a plan for everyone; we just have to be accessible and have faith the size of a mustard seed. As I stood in my kitchen, preparing breakfast for my boys, I wondered if God meant me, Chanel Rye, a stripper from the Hudson Projects. I had done some foul deeds in my life, but only time would tell if I was ready to change or if I was stuck in this lifestyle, cursed by my mother's sins.

Black

I sat in my room, listening to Tupac's "Hail Mary." This was my shit. I wondered if I would ever find my true calling in life. I felt that at thirty years of age, I could be running out of time. After a mountain of dead-end jobs, I had begun thinking that maybe my fate was just to be a regular person living from paycheck to paycheck. However, I seemed to have something deep within that yearned for something more fulfilling. My government name is Sunshine Alezea Rye, but I earned the nickname Black from my beautiful, dark skin tone. I had skin tone the color of coal, dark brown eyes, and a smile that could light up a room. My body was banging as well, but I didn't dwell on that because I was somewhat of a tomboy.

I had been given the nickname Black by my mother, Earlene. I hated it at first, but as time healed old wounds, the name grew on me and became my trademark. I rolled over in my bed and pulled the covers over my head. I needed to get a little more sleep before I had to report to my damn assignment and punch a damn clock. I was currently a cop and working undercover as a detention officer at the correctional facility located just on the outskirts of Millville. I hated undercover work, but putting people away for long periods of time brought me a rush that I could not explain.

In a matter of minutes, the only sounds that could be heard in my room were Tupac and my snoring.

"Uhh," I said as I rolled over and hit the

snooze button on the alarm. I needed fifteen more minutes. I moaned rather loudly. I finally jumped out of bed after coming to my senses and jetted to the bathroom to shower to get my day started. Forty-five minutes later, I was ready and heading to my Jeep (limited edition)—color black, of course—to make this fifty minute drive to the Millville State Prison to begin my twelve hour shift as a detention officer, or glorified babysitter for grown men who have broken the law, and sit around waiting for the mama or baby mama to put money on their books for commissary. The shit was ridiculous to me, but if they liked it, I loved it. I finally pulled up into the employee parking garage to park. I said a quick prayer and exited my Jeep to head to the prison entrance.

"Black, Black," I heard someone scream, and I knew who the hell it was before I even turned around in the direction of the screaming. I turned in the direction of the screaming, prepared to start cussing because I hated when people called my name out in public. I saw Bre Watkins waving her arms around like she was crazy. I just shook my head and waited until she caught up with me. This bitch wore her uniform so damn tight that she could barely move. I knew she suffered of consistent yeast infections. She was ugly as hell, but her body was on point and she was the type that was super thirsty for attention. I guess she was comfortable getting it in however she could. Bre was the workplace gossip queen and knew everybody's business, so I needed her as an ally. I was standing there, waiting for her, wondering what this bitch could want with me now before our shift had even begun. I just rolled my eyes and continued waiting because she was taking her sweet time to get to me.

"Watkins, what the hell do you want?" I asked her when her slow ass finally made it to where I was standing.

"Girrrlll, guess what?" she began.

"What?" I said. "Whose business you about to spill now?"

Laughing at our exchange, we both entered the building to head to briefing and begin this long ass twelve hour shift we had to deal with these damn inmates.

Kee-Kee

I sat nervously in my office, waiting to meet with my new client, Samuel McWalters. Samuel McWalters was his government name, but the streets had christened him Murderville, a play on the hometown name Millville. Samuel was the local drug kingpin. The rumor around town was that he had built a drug empire that generated millions per day. I didn't give a damn about that because M-Ville had been my childhood sweetheart and, as quiet as it was kept, I still loved him from afar for a while. I wondered how this appointment was going to turn out. The freak in me was hoping for sex on my desk, but the professional was hoping that I could just keep it together to handle business and gain a new client. Since I had become a defense attorney, I had prided myself on maintaining my integrity and avoiding street thugs as clients. I had tried to focus on white-collar crimes, fraud, and Ponzi schemes in my practice. As a matter of fact, these defense cases had become my specialty of late and I was living pretty well on the money earned from them as well.

As of late, I had been feeling as though I was lacking excitement and that rush one would get in the courtroom from a high-profile case. So when M-Ville called, that goody two shoes shit went out the window, and I could not resist meeting with him to see what was up. I was thinking that defending a client like M-Ville was just what the doctor ordered to get me out of this funk I seemed to be in, and get my groove back in my professional life. At that very moment, the smell of Dolce & Gabbana Light Blue infiltrated my nostrils and interrupted my private thoughts.

I looked up in the direction of the intoxicating smell, and there stood a gorgeous specimen of a man. I took a quick inventory of the man that stood before me in my office doorway.

Six feet, two inches of chocolate skin that was smooth as butter and 250 pounds of muscle everywhere. He stood there smiling from ear to ear, exposing straight white teeth and dimples, making me extremely wet. Not to mention I was turned on by dimples on an attractive man. Mr. McWalters was dressed to the nines as well: black Armani suit tailored to fit everywhere that mattered, with matching accessories right on down to the Rolex watch he was rocking. Yaass hunty, this man was sexy as hell, and I was not thinking about nothing professional at the moment. Mr. McWalters smelled and looked like money. I was definitely impressed. This sexy motherfucker cleared his throat and said,

"Hello, Ms. Rye. Long time no see. Are you ready to handle my business?"

Now by this time, I could hardly contain myself. I mumbled,

"Yeah, I'll handle your business aight, Mr. McWalters. Umph, umph, umph."

Mr. Sexy Man chuckled and asked, "What was that?"

I snapped out of my little fantasy, cleared my throat, and as professionally as I could, responded with,

"Come right in and have a seat, Mr. McWalters. Let's begin this initial consultation to see if indeed I will be taking you on as a client and handling your business as you say."

I wanted to keep this relationship between us strictly business, but in the back of my mind, something was telling me that it was damn near impossible for that to happen. There was too much chemistry between us for that to happen, but it was a nice thought. I only had two options, personal or professional, and I felt in my heart and my mind that choosing would be hard to do.

Co-Co

I entered Club Body, ready to get my shift started and over with. I was not feeling this shit tonight. I saw that the club was crowded and jumping, as was usual on a Saturday night. Damn, the crowd was all the way turnt up tonight, and seeing this kinda lightened my mood a little. As I turned to head back to the dressing room area, I heard my name being called. "Co-Co, Co-Co!"

I turned in the direction of the yelling and saw the club owner, Davidson, waving his arms and running in my direction. I shook my head. *Damn, this motherfucker gets on my nerves with his stinky ass.* "Hey, diva," he began, all dry and nasty manlike. I chuckled a little under my breath. I was thinking he was probably feeling salty 'cause a while back, he tried to holla and I shot that ass down with quickness. Ole nasty ass! I thought I just threw up in my mouth at the thought of any romantic contact with this ole man Davidson. This man kinda puts you in the mind of the security man on the *Martin* show—straight, nasty-looking with the yuck mouth.

"Hey, Peaches canceled her set tonight, so I'ma . . . uhh, uhh . . . need you to be the main attraction tonight," Davidson was saying when I finally tuned back into the conversation.

"Is this something you can handle, Ms. Dime Diva?" he continued somewhat sarcastically.

"Why, hell yes, Ms. Dime Diva stays ready, so get ready to be entertained!" I replied.

I was so excited to be the main attraction. I had been waiting for this opportunity, and I was going to make the best of it. I turned to walk toward the dressing room, and I added a shake in my walk because I knew his little old ass would be watching and drooling. As I got to the doorway of the dressing room, I turned around and, indeed, he was totally tuned in, so I dropped it like it was hot and gave my ass a little shake.

"Good lawd!" he screamed.

I was too tickled as I got up and rushed into the dressing area to begin preparation for my show. As I entered the dressing area designated for the strippers, I could hear laughter and loud talking, so it seemed that the other girls were in good spirits. Thank goodness, because this meant that no one was tripping and egos were in check. No ass whippings would have to be handed out when the atmosphere was light and cheery. I was so turned up I screamed at the top of my lungs,

"Let's get this money! Let's go, bitches!" Tonight, I had decided to wear my Wonder Woman outfit: short tight blue shorts with stars included that fit my big, voluptuous ass like a second skin. I was the headliner tonight, and I planned to make it count so these thirsty-ass niggas in here would make it rain in this bitch. The only thing on my mind was getting this money, baby. *So please watch me work.* I sat down to apply my makeup and finish getting ready.

This was my first time headlining in Club Body, and I was excited. I finally looked down to check the time; it was 11:55 p.m. It was about showtime, so I made my way to the edge of the stage to wait for my music to begin. Soon the DJ started spinning "Milkshake" by Kelis, and that was my cue to hit the stage. Once on the stage, I could see that the club was still jumping. I began seductively grinding and ass shaking, and the dollars began to rain. All I could think was getting this money, and I put my grinding and shaking into overdrive. I was in top form tonight. I finished my set, collected my dollars, and danced offstage all the way to the dressing room. I was excited from the rush of the stage and my performance. Yass! I did that!

Black

I was beyond tired as I pulled up in the driveway of my house. I had, for some reason, volunteered for a double shift, and it was finally over. All I wanted to do right now was sleep. As I made my way to the front door, my other cell phone rang. I shook my head because I already knew who would be on the other end once I answered the phone. The thought of ignoring it crossed my mind, but I knew there would be hell to pay if I did that. So I answered the damn phone.

"Agent 2211," I said into the receiver.

"Agent 2211, this is Sergeant Mack, we need to have a meeting at 1400 at the secret meeting place to discuss our case."

I wanted to protest, but instead I replied with "Yes sir," and disconnected the phone call. This working undercover was getting on my damn nerves, but I was trying to advance my career. I knew one damn thing, though: I would be glad when this Murderville operation was done and over.

Kee-Kee

I had decided, against my better judgment, to take McWalters on as a client. All my previous clients had been lightweight and low profile compared to Murderville, but maybe the attention this trial was to receive would be just the thing I needed to revive my love for practicing law. This case and this man totally intrigued me, and I absolutely could not resist even if I wanted to. I somewhat knew that the line between business and pleasure was about to be a tricky one to walk because the feelings I was experiencing had me on edge. To be real, I was secretly hoping that our past relationship could be reignited, and I knew the sex would be as good as I last remembered. I also knew I would be facing an uphill battle because of the reputation of a no-nonsense businessman that Murderville had built in the streets.

People feared this man, and you do not have a nickname like Murderville from being nice and polite. I began to look over the charges that my client was facing, and the shit did not look pretty. The State had been trying to collar McWalters for a long time, and they could never get anything to stick. The charges that I was looking at kind of scared me a bit because if he were convicted this time, he would most definitely not see the light of day again. The list of charges read like this: distribution, drug trafficking, kidnapping, terroristic threats, attempted murder, and bribery of a public official. Good lord!

I immediately got a headache from reading all that shit and wondering if I had bitten off more than I could chew with taking this man on as a client. I had my work cut out for me. I was looking over the evidence that the prosecution had to see how I would be defending my client in this case. I made up my mind that losing was not an option for me or my ego. McWalters had made it clear that losing was not an option for him either because he had no plans of spending the rest of his life behind bars. What laid on the horizon, I did not know, but I did know that things could certainly get very ugly.

I hoped I could handle the ride. I began to prepare for my second meeting with Mr. McWalters, and I knew that the situation could get intense. The charges that he was facing were serious business, and the prosecution was looking for blood. They also wanted to make an example out of my client for his misdeeds and crimes against the community and the citizens of Millville. I knew that had anyone else besides Murderville walked into my office looking for representation, I would have declined taking on their case.

The prosecution had no concrete evidence of my client committing crimes or dealing drugs. All their evidence was circumstantial and based on hearsay testimony from criminals linked to my client and his organization, so I knew for sure that I would start by demolishing the testimony of the prosecution's witnesses. My competitive instincts kicked in, and I was determined not to lose this case for both professional and personal reasons.

Co-Co

I was still riding on a high from last night, being the headliner and making the amount of money that I made for one night. I rolled over and grabbed my stash from dancing and began to count it all over again. I still could not believe that I had $5,000 in my hands. *Ballin'! This is the life.* I took the money and threw it up in the air. A bitch like me could get used to this kind of money on a daily basis, and I knew I could, for sure, move the fuck out the projects on this kind of money as well.

So, I began to wonder how the hell I could move up the ranks at Club Body with quickness. I needed to headline more than just one time. I needed to do this shit on the regular. Maybe I needed to pay Davidson the attention he was looking for and break him off a little something, something. I shuddered at the thought of sexing his nasty ole ass, but to get what you want out of life, sacrifices need to be made. In any event, whatever plan I came up with, I knew it had to be flawless, because my livelihood and the livelihood of my children were at stake. Team main event was in full effect, but right now, I was about to take my children out on the town.

"Ray-Ray, Juju, where y'all at?" I was screaming through this little-ass apartment.

"Y'all get up and get dressed so we can go and spend this money! Let's go!"

Black

I pulled up to the designated meeting place, which was an inconspicuous warehouse in the midst of the downtown club scene. I used my security badge to enter the building. The team had already assembled; as usual, I was the last to arrive.

"Hello, guys," I said, entering the room.

"Let's get this show on the road so I can return home to my comfy bed and get some damn sleep."

I was slightly irritated. Team M-Ville, as we had deemed ourselves, consisted of me, Agent 2211; Sergeant Mack; Sergeant Williams (team leads); and Officers Daniels, 2311; Stevens, 2411;

and Bills, 2511. This was a team assembled to end the drug epidemic in Millville and take down the drug kingpin Samuel McWalters. Recently, there had been an influx of drugs turning up in the local prison, and that was why I was undercover as a detention officer at the moment to help get to the root of the problem and bring the organization to its knees. Rumor on the streets was that McWalters was behind the drug ring inside Millville State Prison. The one mission of this team was to catch Murderville with his fingers in the cookie jar and reclaim the streets of Millville for its citizens. My team and I had committed to the cause of doing whatever it took to accomplish our goal of cleaning up the drug problem in Millville and putting behind bars the scumbags that were dealing and selling the drugs as well. Sergeant Mack was briefing the team on new developments on the case.

"Okay, team," he began,

"The DA plans to indict Samuel 'Murderville' McWalters within the next few weeks. The evidence is circumstantial, so hopefully soon we can add something of substance to the State's case to make the charges stick and allow them to put this motherfucker behind bars for a long-ass time."

"To date," he continued, "the charges are as follows: distribution, drug trafficking, attempted murder, terroristic threat, and bribery of a public official. My informant says that Murderville has hands in the drugs that are entering the state prison, so we can definitely add that to the charges if it proves to be true."

Sergeant Mack then turned in my direction and said, "So, Agent Rye, do you have any information to add to the briefing today?"

I stood up and said, "At this particular point, I am still getting acquainted with the system. I have made some promising contacts within the system and with the inmates that are connected to what is currently happening."

"And also," I continued, "I have come into some information that leads me to believe that one or more of the detention officers may be involved with this drug ring and bringing contraband into the prison facility as well."

"One last thing I want to add," I said, "this thing is huge, and it involves a hell of a lot of people that are connected in high places."

"What do you mean by that?" Sergeant Mack asked.

"I mean that people in high places and positions, from the top to the bottom, are about to be exposed and taken down. From the highest to the lowest, things are about to get ugly, and when the smoke clears, some very prominent citizens in Millville will be in very hot water." I laughed out loud.

"The shit is about to hit the fan, and I cannot wait to see who will be exposed and who will be left standing."

I could not wait to bust Murderville's dirty ass, and this was personal. I needed to pay back this piece of shit for tricking my mother, turning her out, and then doing the same shit to my sister Co-Co. Oh yes, this shit was most definitely personal. We went over some more trivial stuff about our operation and the team, and then Sergeant Mack ended the meeting by telling us to be careful and professional in all interactions with the public. The meeting finally ended, and I headed home to get some much needed sleep. Boy, was I tired! I was so exhausted, and by now, my head was pounding. I might need to rethink my career choice once this undercover investigation was over. Right now, though, I was going to get some z's. My bed was currently calling my name, and I was about to answer. I retreated to my room once I made it home and crawled under the covers, and before my head hit the pillow, I would be down for the count.

Mikeela

I was in the process of putting the finishing touches on one of my other clients' case so that I would be free to pay full attention to Murderville and his case. I was determined to not let anything distract me or get in my way of obtaining victory. I felt as though if I won this case, Mr. Sexy Ass McWalters would worship the ground I walked on. The criminal case that the prosecution had was a good circumstantial case, but it was not a sure win. I needed to demolish the witnesses' testimony and make sure that there was no secret somewhere waiting to blindside me. I had been thinking that since the majority of the witnesses for the prosecution were former acquaintances of McWalters and criminals in their own right, showing them in a negative light would be a piece of cake. The prosecution had sent a partial list of the witnesses that they planned to have on the stand, and I wanted to go over the list with Samuel to gain a better understanding of the relationship that he, the client, had with each witness. This tactic, I hoped, would allow for me to prepare a defense and a line of questioning that would destroy their credibility with the judge and the jury. I had learned just yesterday that, indeed, the grand jury had decided to indict McWalters, so it was game time and there was no room for errors. I pressed the speaker button on the intercom and said,

"Mrs. Wallace, please contact Mr. McWalters and arrange for a meeting tomorrow at a convenient time for both parties to discuss some particulars on his case."

"Yes, ma'am. Ms. Rye, I will schedule that appointment right away," Mrs. Wallace replied to me through the intercom.

In the short time that I had decided to take Samuel McWalters on as a client, I had learned that he had been arrested on suspicion of organized crime. He had posted bail and came immediately to my office after firing his lifetime attorney, Sand White. The word on the street was that Sand White skipped town soon after. I had no idea if it was on his own accord or not. The answer to that question was still a mystery. I shook my suspicions from my mind. I had a case to win, so preparation was a must. The only agenda I had on my mind at this moment was winning. Winning the case and winning the man.

"Ms. Rye," I heard over the intercom, which scared the shit out of me.

"Yes," I replied after I recovered from being startled.

"Mr. McWalters will be in at 2:00 p.m. tomorrow."

"Okay, great," I replied.

"And don't schedule anyone for the next couple of weeks. I am giving Mr. McWalters and this case my full- time attention."

"Ten-four," replied Mrs. Wallace.

I continued to busy myself with the preparations for my meeting with Samuel tomorrow all the way down to the outfit I was going to wear. Everything had to be perfect and in order. My game face was on, and Operation Win Samuel McWalters was now in full effect.

Co-Co

I really enjoyed taking my boys out shopping. I loved the smiles on their faces while they were picking out outfits and shoes to wear. Life in the projects sometimes did not afford many luxuries, but when the opportunity presented itself to splurge a little, that was exactly what I intended to do. One thing's for certain, two things for sure, if I had my way, my children and I would not be living the project life for much longer. I had been saving my money, and moving to a better neighborhood for the good of my children was the first thing on my agenda of things to do. I grew up in the projects where I was currently residing, and I craved for a better living environment for my children.

On the way home, I stopped by a local restaurant so that my boys, Juju and Ray-Ray, could play on the little playground inside the place and enjoy some food. I allowed the boys to play a bit so I could be alone to think about the next move I was going to make. I needed a plan to accomplish my goal of leaving the strip club and the projects behind once and for all. Despite my upbringing and the decisions I had made, I was not going to let my children suffer like I had because of the choices of my mother. I just was not sure if I could do what needed to be done without using my looks and my body. However, if my body was what I had to use to get to where I wanted to be, then that was what I would do. After all, it was my specialty and what I had been trained to do.

"Oh well, by any means necessary," I said aloud to no one in particular. Before going to the restaurant, I had stopped by the local convenience store to pick up a newspaper to read while the kids played. The hot gossip on the street and around Club Body was that Samuel McWalters, a.k.a. Murderville, was in hot water, and I wanted to read the article and get details on what the locals thought they knew. I knew one thing: I hoped that he'd finally get what he deserved. Time would soon tell, and I could not wait, because karma is a bitch and she certainly dealt the best revenge.

The history between the two of us was brief, but it existed. The shit had left me battered and bruised with a bad taste in my mouth. I did not know how to feel while preparing to read this article, and the bastard's name being mentioned had me all up in my feelings. I was definitely feeling some type of way. I needed a stiff drink. I sat at the corner table close to the playground so that I would be able to keep an eye on the boys. I opened up the newspaper and began reading the article. The headline read, *"The Indictment of Samuel 'Murderville' McWalters, the man that all of Millville feared."* I continued to read, and my heart stopped:

Reports indicate that Mr. Samuel McWalters has fired his longtime counsel, Sand White, and obtained local hotshot criminal defense attorney Mikeela Denise Rye. I was totally speechless! My very own sister was representing the enemy. So much for loyalty! So much for blood was thicker than water. I had not spoken to my sisters Mikeela and Sunshine in a few years, but surely, Kee-Kee remembered all the drama that McWalters had caused in my life and the lives of our family. I knew that if this bitch had forgotten, I was going to make it a point to give her a quick refresher course to remind the high and mighty lawyer the true meaning of *loyalty*. I knew Kee-Kee had always been thirsty when it came to dick, but this was fucking ridiculous. I could not do anything else but shake my head and feel betrayed.

Black

I was startled from a deep sleep. I jumped up to my feet and began to pace back and forth nonstop for some reason. I had an uneasy feeling that there was something major on the horizon that had the potential to change lives, if not end them. Damn, I should have rethought this undercover operation—but it wasn't like I had a choice in the matter. I was from the projects, the ghetto, and I knew if word got out about my being a police officer, the repercussions could be deadly. Everyone knew the universal code of the hood: snitches get stitches. The ole heads in the neighborhood had gone crazy when they learned that I was working as a detention officer at the state prison, so I could only imagine what the reaction would be when the true nature of my involvement in this investigation against Murderville would come to light.

Murderville was a hood legend, and people loved this nigga. I tried shaking off my thoughts by going into the kitchen to pour myself a glass of Crown and Coke to calm my nerves. I drank that shit in one good gulp. I thought that maybe a good, long, hot shower would help as well. I eventually made my way to the bathroom and turned on the hot water in the shower. I immediately removed my clothes and stepped in. The moment the water hit my body, my mind began to relax and I felt I could finally get a good night's sleep. I knew that soon my personal and professional lives would eventually come to a head. I just hoped I was ready for the consequences and that I was on the winning side, still standing.

Kee-Kee

I had the meeting with McWalters, and it went rather well. However, I could not shake the feeling that he was not telling the total truth. I knew that surprises in a case like this could surely determine that I'd end up losing and my client spending the rest of his natural life behind bars. I planned to iterate the importance of trust between attorney and client. I wanted to be sure that he knew the full consequences of withholding information from me and having the opposing team blindside me with it in the midst of the trial.

McWalters had asked me out to dinner, and despite the professional ramifications, I accepted. However, I planned to address my concerns about what he said to be the truth regarding the case and the charges brought against him to get that out of the way and put my mind at ease. I wanted to enjoy this night out with a man. It had been a disaster the last time I was out, and I deserved to be treated and given some male attention. My mind had told me to decline, but my vagina said I needed to go. So considering the fact that I was planning for the dinner date, you can guess who I chose to listen to.

Lawd have mercy! I hope I am not getting into something that I will not be able to handle.

I shook those thoughts from my mind and began to get ready for my dinner date with Mr. Sexy. I planned to make him pay attention to more than my law degree tonight. Shit, wrong or right, I wanted to make a love connection. Once upon a time, back in the Hudson projects, the two of us shared feelings, and I was wondering if we would be able to recapture that connection yet again. I knew that back in the day, McWalters was my first love but I went to college to escape the projects and he got lost in the streets. I had clothes thrown all over the place in my bedroom. I was searching for the perfect outfit, and for some reason, I was a ball of nerves.

This man made me feel a way that I had not felt regarding a man in a long time. I believed I had the love jones. I did not know how I felt about the way I was feeling about a man that represented something so different from what I represented. But every good girl is always in search of a bad boy, and since childhood project days, Murder had been my chosen bad boy. I eventually decided on a black-and-white tuxedo dress that fit my curves in all the right places and sat on my ass just the way I liked. I chose some black Louboutin stilettos. I sprayed on my favorite cologne, Ralph Lauren Romance. A lady should always look and smell like a lady. Before leaving my room to go downstairs, I did a once-over in the full-length mirror. I had to admit, I was on fleek and my body was snatched in this outfit I had chosen. I took a deep breath to relax because I currently had this man on my mind. The things I was thinking was making me crazy.

As I made my way down the stairs, I heard the doorbell ring. I wondered who the hell that could be 'cause I didn't have time for any drama tonight. I didn't bother asking who it was. I just opened the damn door with as much attitude as I could muster, ready to cuss whomever was on the other side out. How dare they come to my house without calling, trying to hinder my plans! I looked up and there he stood, as fine as wine. Damn, my mood soon changed with quickness. He smelled so delicious. Forget soup; shit, McWalters was umm, umm *good*!

I finally regained my composure and said in the sexiest tone I could, "What a surprise! I thought I was meeting you at De Lamar's tonight." McWalters said in a sexy baritone, "I am a gentleman at all times, so it's only natural that I take charge and take care of all aspects of a date that I asked you out on. So if you have no more questions, madame, your chariot awaits." He stepped aside, and I saw a beautiful stretched limo waiting to take us to dinner. I could get used to this shit! I was smiling from ear to ear as I made my way to the limo.

Co-Co

I was still feeling uneasy about my sister Mikeela (Kee-Kee) representing Murderville in his criminal case. I had decided to let sleeping dogs lie for the moment because I wanted to have all my ducks in a row before I tackled this issue with my lovely sister. In the meantime, money needed to be made, so I began to prepare my mind to shake my ass and collect these coins. I was on next. I did a quick glance in the mirror to make sure that everything was in its proper place. After agreeing that it was, I made my way to the edge of the stage and waited for the DJ to play my song. I did a few last-minute stretches to make sure that thing was right and on point.

For some reason, tonight we had an announcer, and she was in the process of introducing me with her corny ass. I hated when we had an announcer, cause it fucked with my rhythm and timing of my music. And this corny-ass bitch was saying, "The moment you have been waiting for, last night's main attraction, Co-Co 'the Rump Shaker' Ryeee!" I made my way to the center of the stage, shaking my assets to wreck in effect. Rump Shaker. The dollar bills began to rain and litter the stage. I was excited 'cause judging from the money hitting the stage, tonight was gonna be a good night.

Upon completing my dance, I began to collect my money from the stage, and as I was about to get the last one-hundred-dollar bill from the edge of the stage, someone from my blind side grabbed by wrist. I was shocked as hell, and I started to immediately go off. "You grimly, low-class motherfucker, you better let go of my —" I fell silent because I looked into the eyes of who held my wrist and I was scared shitless. A blast from the past stood before me, Michael MD Williams, and he was smiling from ear to ear. I was scared to death because it seemed that my past had finally come back to haunt me.

MD slid close to my face and whispered in my ear, "Long time no see. I have a message from the boss. Murderville would like to see you to tie up some loose ends, you know, old business. He would like for it to be sooner rather than later, and it would also be best for you and your family if you came on your own accord, 'cause if I gotta hunt you down, there will be consequences to pay. Keep your eyes and ears open because we will be in touch with the particulars for the meeting, and discretion is in your best interest."

He then dropped five one-hundred-dollar bills on the stage and said, "One hell of a show! You still can shake that ass with the best of them." He winked and strutted off. I was at a loss for words. I had no idea what the hell just happened or what the hell was about to happen. I was numb with fear and shaken to my core. How I made it back to the dressing room, I had no idea. I was so scared that I waited in the club until the sun came up before I left and went to my car. I sure was praying that my ass would not be swimming with the fish anytime soon.

Black

I awoke to a ringing cell phone. I decided to ignore it. I was off for four days, and today, I didn't want to talk to anyone or deal with any drama. I rolled back over and decided to go right back to sleep. I was so drained, and today was as good as any to sleep in.

"Noo, noo, noo!" I was screaming as I shot straight up in the bed. I soon noticed that I was also dripping with sweat.

"Ohh my god!" I said into an empty bedroom, heaving as I raised my hands to my face. I was literally shaking uncontrollably.

"Man, that dream I just had seemed so real."

I only hoped it did not come to fruition. I decided to jump in the shower to calm my nerves and freshen up a bit. I could not, for some reason, shake the dream I just had. I had just dreamed that I was on the run from Murderville and his goons. He was trying to kill me, my sisters, and my mother. I hadn't dealt with Murderville personally in years. When I left the Hudson projects, I left behind the people, the problems, and the stress that came with project living. Murderville had been bad news from the womb. He hadn't brought anything to the Hudson projects and my family but drama. I hated this man with a passion for what he had turned my mother, Earlene, into. Murderville took it upon himself to trick my mother on the streets and control her with crack, which became her drug of choice and her life.

Before my mother became a hoe and a crackhead, she had been the best mother in the world. We were not rich, but we were happy. My mother had dreams of leaving the projects for a better life. She had started taking college courses with a transitional state program, and everything seemed promising. Then one night, she didn't come home, and that one night turned into a week. When she finally did reappear, my sister and I had been in the apartment for a week with no food and the damn lights had been turned off. Mikeela was four, I was one, and Co-Co was not born yet. I was young, but I knew the moment I laid eyes on my mother that our life would never be the same again.

My mother was a crackhead, and she did whatever to get that next high. For a high and a fix, our very own mother had sacrificed her children's innocence and the little stability that we had living in the projects. That was why when I got my chance to run, I did and I did not look back. I was not sure but, I believed that Murderville had even tricked out my little sister, Co-Co. I had left her behind because she was already running in the streets and, at that time, no one could tame her. I was thinking about my survival, and I was not sure if that was the right decision to be made. I think my sisters and I had all suffered from the environment the projects provided. Maybe one day we could make amends and start the healing process to put our family back together again. Only God knew the answer. Even though my sisters and I lived in the same city, we had not spoken to one another in at least five years.

I shook my head back and forth because that really didn't make any damn sense. Right now, that was the reality of the relationship that we had. I was thinking that Murderville was the last person I wanted to have a problem with in the streets, because the streets were his territory. He owned the projects and the drug scene. I knew that it would be hard to find anyone to turn over on him, due to the way he delivered street justice to those he deemed unloyal.

Though I did not want to deal with Murderville face-to-face on the streets, there was a part of me that wanted revenge. I also knew that my undercover assignment and my profession would soon lead to me clashing with the goon squad, and I was going to make damn sure that I was ready. When the smoke cleared, I was sure that I would be left standing. I eventually got around to checking my missed calls, and I had one. The name read Chanel. I shook my head back and forth again. Here we went with the drama, because Co-Co only called when she was caught up in some shit or wanted something. The very reason why I hadn't talked to her ass in a minute.

Mikeela

I felt on the other side of my bed. Yep, he was still there. Last night was amazing. I was smiling from ear to ear and whistling and shit. I was happy as hell! It really had been a minute since I had done the deed with a man. Of course, I had my little battery-operated friend, but that was not the same as being with a man.

I decided to wash up and head to the kitchen to fix some breakfast for Mr. McWalters. My happy ass danced all the way down the stairs to the kitchen. While I began cooking, I replayed last night's events over in my head.

Murderville and I had left my house in a limo and arrived at De Lamar's at around 8:30 p.m. To my surprise, he had rented out the whole restaurant and we had been the only ones in the place besides the staff. The plan had been to discuss the case, but we had gotten sidetracked by reminiscing about old times and old feelings. The case took a backseat for the moment. Dinner was delicious, and the romantic gesture of renting out the restaurant was a hit with me. There had been a lot of laughter, drinks, and flirting going on at the table. One thing led to another and no one wanted the night to end, so I invited him in for a nightcap.

By the end of the nightcap, hell, we ended up in my bed, getting it in. "Good morning, Kee-Kee!" Murderville said, scaring the shit out of me.

"Oh my god," I said, turning around,

"you scared me, Samuel!" I playfully hit him on the hand. Damn, this man was so sexy to me.

"I get breakfast too," he said, smiling that smile that made me melt and my panties wet.

I replied, "It's the least I could do after your performance last night."

I put the finishing touches on the breakfast, prepared our plates, and set them on the table. "I had planned on serving breakfast in bed, but since you decided to come downstairs, I guess we're eating at the kitchen table," I said to Murderville.

"Well, I prefer eating in the kitchen. It makes the conversation I want to have with you easier for you to comprehend," he said. "Last night was great," he continued. "Sex was on point. You most definitely did your thang in them sheets, but I need for you to understand that it was just that for me—sex. The only relationship that you and I will ever have is professional. So I don't need for you catching feelings over one sexual encounter and lose focus on what your job for me is. You, Mikeela, are hired help. I hired you to be my lawyer, and that is where your main focus needs to be, 'cause if you lose this case, it would be really bad for you and those you care about."

This motherfucker said all this while sitting in my house and eating my damn food. I was stunned, and apparently, he was not finished because he was still talking. "It is just sex, and I have no romantic feelings for you. I am and will forever be married to the streets and getting this money. Females ain't loyal, love ain't loyal, and it damn sure don't live here, so I suggest you get your mind right and focus on the job you were hired to do. You have no time to be playing house," Murderville said.

He got up to head back upstairs and turned around to add a cherry on top of what he had just said. "The sex was on point, but the only way it can continue is if you can separate the pleasure from the business by understanding that business will always remain most important. My motto is "Business over bullshit." And with that, he turned and retreated up the steps. I didn't know what the fuck to think or how to react. I didn't know if I was more disturbed by what Murderville had just said or by the fact that I was actually contemplating whether or not I could live with his terms. Was I really that damn desperate? Was I really that thirsty? I was leaning toward yes 'cause Samuel "Murderville" McWalters still knew how to rock my body after all these years.

Co-Co

I was still disturbed by the visit I received from Murderville's main enforcer, MD, a.k.a. Mad Dawg. I had thought that my dealings with that part of my life were over. Sometimes I would lose myself in thoughts about my childhood. I remember when I was fourteen years of age and I decided I was grown and I ran away from my grandmother's house.

At that time, my sisters and I had been living with grandmother Hattie Allen. My granny was a great woman of God who provided for us the best she could. I was young, dumb, and rebellious. I thought I was grown and no one could tell me shit. I had been living on my terms all my life and rules and regulations cramped my style, so I packed my belongings and hit the streets. The little money I had at that time ran out really fast. I wandered into an after-hours club, begging for food and water. This would be my first encounter with Murderville up close and personal. I had seen him around the way and roaming the projects, but I never paid him any mind and I never knew his name. After all, I was only a child. Murderville had been nice and considerate that night. He fed me and offered me a place to clean up and get a good night's sleep. If I knew then what I know now, I would have continued on my way, 'cause it's true what they say: nothing in life is free.

I remembered that him being so nice made me feel so safe for the first time in my young life. However, that feeling would be short-lived 'cause as soon as morning came, the man I came to know as Mad Dawg (MD) burst into the room I was sleeping in and demanded that I dress and report downstairs in thirty minutes. I was so young and naive. Frightened, confused, and discombobulated, I still managed to do as I was told and reported downstairs.

Once I was downstairs, I saw a handsome young man pacing back and forth. He had on gold chains and diamond rings. The B-boy vibe was in full effect with this dude, and I was informed by MD that his name was Murderville and I would be doing whatever the hell he wanted me to do. I did not have the option of saying no. I remember Murder turning to me and beginning reciting to me everything that was required of me in order to repay him for the room and board that he had so graciously given me.

At that time in the game, Murder had a scheme in play in which he used pretty young girls to lure men into sexual encounters. Once the men took the bait, he would send his goons in the room and rob the men, who were none the wiser. So, because I had accepted a meal and a place to lay my head in, I became a young ass bait whore by default. Murderville was a young and upcoming nigga in the drug game at the time I had been so lucky to encounter his presence.

So, like I mentioned before, at fourteen years old, I was a bait girl for Murder's organization, but this gig soon switched from setting men up in hotel rooms to me strolling the street corner, turning tricks, just like mommy dearest. I had seen a lot of dirt done by Murderville and his team of goons, and I could only imagine what he wanted to talk with me about. I shook my head back and forth to somehow try to shake the thought from my mind as I wiped the tears from my eyes. Those memories were still so painful, and I hated to rehash them. *Damn, what does Murder want?*

He had already done major damage to my life. Why was he still trying to inflict pain? To make matters worse, my stupid-ass sister Kee-Kee was representing this fool in his case! I knew Mikeela was probably still sweet on this nigga. My sister Mikeela would do anything for Murderville then and now. The shit was just ratchet. Straight ratchet. This drama that was developing was too much for me, so I just decided to stay in bed the rest of the day. The memories of my tricking and licking were way too much for me to handle for right now. I was totally over this damn day already.

Black

I wondered what Co-Co wanted with me. I hadn't spoken with my sister in a month of Sundays. I was almost certain that it had to do with the Murderville drama. Co-Co was a stripper, and she always brought drama wherever she went. Because of that one reason, I had decided a long time ago to keep my distance until she chose to do better regarding her life decisions. My family was an embarrassment that I wanted to not interfere with my professional or current personal life. I actually loved my sisters, but I just could not get past the fact that Co-Co had reduced herself to turning tricks and, now stripping. She went from sucking dick to shaking ass just to get a quick buck. I often wondered if Co-Co's choosing to strip was really an improvement in her eyes.

Mikeela, my other sister, was so bourgeois she would swear that her shit doesn't stink. The rumor on the street was that Kee-Kee was representing Murderville in his upcoming trial. I knew that Kee-Kee was going to always have a thing for Murder because he was her first love, but he was also responsible for destroying our family unit. Because Murder had brainwashed one sister, turned one sister into a young whore, and made my mother a crack whore, I had a personal vendetta to settle with the motherfucker and I didn't plan on taking any prisoners. Win lose or draw, I vowed to make Murder's dirty ass pay the piper for the crimes he committed against my family and my community.

Family—you can't live with them and you can't live without them, but you can keep their ass at a distance if they continue to make fucked up decisions. All this thinking about my family and Murderville had my damn head hurting, so I decided to go for a run to clear my mind. Running always calmed me down when I was becoming overly emotional. During the third mile of my run, I decided to leave the drama with my family on the back burner, but I knew sooner rather than later, I would have to face the issues that we had with one another.

Murderville

I had been pacing back and forth in my home office for what seemed like hours. This conversation I was having with my connect was driving me fucking insane. My connect, Loco, was talking some shit about him not being able to do business with me anymore 'cause I was hot and might bring heat his way. I had been in this game for over thirty years, and he had been my connection for most of those years and I ain't never brought no heat to him or anyone else I broke bread with. This motherfucker was straight tripping, and he was pissing me the fuck off. For real. I had been loyal to Loco and had always had his back. Now he wants to nut up when I had a little drama my way. I hated disloyalty, and if he showed himself disloyal and fucked up my money in any way, I would deal with his ass too.

While I was on the phone, I saw MD walk in. I had sent him to Club Body to deliver a message to that bitch Co-Co. I gave MD a signal to hold on while I finished my convo with Loco bitch-ass. I wanted to meet with Co-Co to let her know that if she just so happened to be a witness in my case, she better develop amnesia about any motherfucking thing she might know about me and my damn business. I knew I had a snitch somewhere in my roster, but I could not put my finger on who it was. I had been doing business with all these niggas for years, so I was not sure who it was, but one thing's for certain I would find him or her.

"Hey, Loco, you know what? I'ma end this conversation right now with you 'cause you talking sideways. I suggest you rethink your position because I never abandoned you in your times of need. And you a bitch if you do me that way. Fuck!" I said, slamming down my trap phone. I shook my head. The game and the streets ain't loyal to no one. Therefore, if you were in the game, it was best that you trust no one. MD sat straight up in his chair, ready to go to war.

"Everything one hun'ed, boss? 'Cause you know I'm always ready to put in work," he said.

"First things first, did you pay a visit to our stripper bitch Ms. Co- Co?"

"Hell yeah!" MD said.

"The message has been delivered, and the chick almost shit herself when she saw me, a ghost from her past. The stripper Co-Co was informed of the fact that you needed to meet with her and that I would be returning with particulars. And from experience, I'm sure she knows that declining is not an option, so now that is covered, what was that phone call about?" MD added, almost all in one breath.

I began, "My connect, Loco, talking shit about he don't know if he can continue business with me 'cause of all the heat and media attention of the upcoming trial. That's number 1. That's who I was on the phone with when you came in, but it's more 'cause before that call, I received two more. Number 2 is Sand White's body has been recovered because it washed up on shore earlier today, and number 3, the Harrisburg connect say they having trouble getting enough product inside the Millville State Prison, so the supply is not meeting the demand, and that's fucking up my money! And getting money is the only thing I love to do continuously."

"Oh shit, when it rains it pours!" MD said.

"So do you want me to find some more guards to put on to handle this problem?" he finished.

"Most def, that needs to be done like yesterday," I replied to MD.

All this shit was making my head hurt, but it was nothing I could not handle. MD pulled out his cell phone and aggressively punched in some numbers and put the phone to his ear.

"Helllloo, Officer Watkins!" MD screamed into the phone. "With your sexy ass, I got some new instructions for you per the boss," he continued." While MD finished up his conversation with Watkins, I went to my bar to pour me a stiff drink and decide what my next move was going to be 'cause I had a feeling that sooner or later, I would be going to war to maintain my way of life. Whoever was coming for me better make damn sure they were ready because I stayed ready and winning was the only thing I knew how to do.

Kee-Kee

I was in my office, preparing my notes on the case concerning Murderville. I was trying to stay focused, but I couldn't stop replaying the sex session between him and me. I also could not forget the conversation that had occurred in my damn kitchen. Had I known he felt that way, I would not have made his ass no damn breakfast. Murder had, in no uncertain terms, revealed that he wanted to be friends with benefits. I was feeling some type of way about that shit, but I decided to let sleeping dogs lie for the moment because business and money come before pleasure. I pressed my intercom and said,

"Mrs. Wallace, can you please get Mad Dawg, or MD, set up for an interview with me as soon as possible? We need to go over testimony and case specifics to make sure everyone concerned is on the same page at the time of trial."

"M-a-d Dawg? I am sure that is not his real name. Really?" my secretary, Mrs. Wallace, replied into the intercom.

I giggled a little and said, "Well no, ma'am, his government name is Michael Williams."

"Now that sounds so much better and a whole lot less threatening, and yes, I will schedule Michael Williams for an appointment with you as soon as possible," my secretary said into the intercom before disconnecting.

I was busy preparing my list of witnesses and was getting discouraged with each name that I added. The list contained nothing but heathens and known criminals. There was Mad Dawg, Murderville's known enforcer, and the streets had christened him Dr. Death. There was Steven Jay, second-in-command, and word on the street was that he secretly wanted to replace Murder. Then there was Rick Nichols; no one really knew what he actually did for a living or his role within the organization, but it must pay very well 'cause this brother stayed bossed up and was pushing a nice, expensive ride. Last but not the least was Beachie, who was a low-level hustler who associated with Murderville, and of course, everyone knew he was a snitch.

I most definitely had my work cut out for me. I needed to find some community leaders who had clean reputations that could testify about some of the good things that my client had contributed to throughout the years. For my sake, I hoped this existed. Surely, there was some type of turkey drive or monetary contributions to organizations that I could use to show my client had done something besides criminal activity in the very community that we had all grown up in. "Damn," I said out loud, "all these motherfuckers on this list shady as hell!"

I felt ill almost instantly, and I had an uneasiness in the pit of my stomach. I threw that damn list to the side for now because it was stressing me out. I then decided to check out the prosecution witness list more closely because when it was first delivered, I really didn't look at it due to the excitement of meeting Samuel and getting reacquainted with him. I scanned the list and was shocked and dumbfounded by one name that stood out in a manner that no other name mattered.

I read the name out loud, "Chanel Rene Rye! What the fuck! My sister is a witness for the prosecution? What on earth did my sister have to tell? What was her connection to Murderville concerning this case?"

I knew my sister was into the street life and that she and Murder had grown up in the same projects, but what could she possibly have to add regarding the charges against my client? Anyways, my sister was a hoe, so as far as I was concerned, her testimony was questionable as well, and if push came to shove, I would destroy that bitch on the witness stand as well.

Co-Co

I hadn't been back to the strip club since the encounter with Mad Dawg. To say that I was terrified would be an understatement. I screamed at the top of my lungs,

"Juuuujuuuu, come herrree!"

"Wat you want?" Juju said, standing at my bedroom door with attitude on his face.

"Who the hell you think you talking too, Ju?" I asked, a little pissed off.

"You," Juju replied.

"Anyway, lil boy, go see if you can see the mailman and get the mail."

"Okay," he said and made a mad dash to the front door.

Five minutes later, Juju came back with the mail. "Here you go, Mama," Juju sang while simultaneously throwing the mail in my direction, and he turned and went running to the front room.

"All right, Juju, I'ma whip yo lil ass!"

I gathered up the mail and prepared to look through it when I heard Juju and Ray-Ray yelling, "Mamma, Mamma. It's a white man at the doe!"

"What the hell!" I said out loud to myself.

Annoyed, I got up and pulled on my duster and went into the front room, and sure enough, there stood the POPO at my damn door. I immediately knew he was law enforcement. He was straight business, not a smile in sight. That was why I hated these motherfuckers. How could you knock at somebody's door and not offer no form of greeting?

Fuck you too, Mr. White Man! I said all this in my head of course as I stood at the door waiting for him to address me.

"Ms. Chanel Rene Rye?" he asked.

"Yes," I said.

"You have been served," he said, and with that

he turned and walked off.

"Well, damn," I said.

I looked at the envelope and ripped it open. It was a subpoena to be a witness for the prosecution in the case against Murderville. I immediately could feel my blood run cold. I could not believe this shit! I could not testify in open court against a hood nigga like Murder and live to talk about it. What in God's name was I gonna do? Testifying would label me a snitch, and I could never show my face again in this damn neighborhood. The whole damn world knew that snitches get stitches in the street or, in this case, snitches just might end up swimming with the fish. It was in this moment that the visit from MD made sense. Shit was beginning to get real.

Black

My head was still spinning. I had just left briefing with the undercover unit. The investigation had led to information that Officer Watkins, a member of the Millville State Prison for fifteen years, was rumored to be on the payroll of Murderville. Not only was this bitch on Murder's payroll, but she was also to be in charge of recruiting new officers into the organization. The plan of the new recruits was to smuggle contraband and narcotics into the prison. The payment of the product had been set up to be collected by Watkins on the outside from the inmates' personal connections.

Apparently, this was a lucrative way to supplement the income of the officers as well as big business for the inmates, and Murderville and his organization of goons. I liked Officer Watkins' noisy ass, but if you couldn't do the time, you should not do the crime. I was going to make sure that I personally arrest this scandalous bitch and whomever she was connected with inside the prison walls. I was damn sure I was going to enjoy doing it. I eventually allowed my mind to drift back to the missed call I had received from my sister Co-Co. I hoped she was not involved in any business with Murderville anymore, because if I had to, I would cuff her ass too. I had no discrimination when it came to upholding the law and doing my job.

Murder had been messing up the lives of the people in my family for way too long. The investigation and takedown of his drug empire was a must. I, for one, could not wait to arrest his ass and see him in prison for the rest of his natural life. I hated this nigga from the time I met him strolling the projects like he owned them so long ago. He had been a troublemaker from birth, a generational gangbanger, and a drug dealer. He was destined to rule the drug game and take over the Hudson projects, and by the looks of it, he had accomplished just that. Murderville's father had been a drug dealer.

Papa V was what everyone had called Murder's father. Murderville and his father had turned my mother into a crackhead and a hoe all at the same damn time. Yes, indeed, they had my mother turning tricks, but my mother really got worse after PapaV died. I think that maybe, Papa V and my mom, Earlene, had a thing for each other, but I was not 100 percent sure about that. I hated what my mother had allowed to happen to her life and the lives of me and my sisters. "Hell yeah, karma is a bitch, and vengeance shall be mine!" I said aloud to myself. I could not wait to serve this motherfucker exactly what he deserved.

Kee-Kee

My head was fucked up from my meeting with Murderville's topman, Michael Williams, a.k.a. Mad Dawg. I had asked him some basic questions about his position within the organization and was given a rehearsed answer. Mad Dawg answered like most street niggas did when questioned by law enforcement or lawyers. The trust was nonexistent even though I was trying to help the team he was on. Mr. Williams had informed me he was simply hired security for Mr. McWalters and he had no firsthand knowledge on his criminal involvement or business dealings within the community. Mad Dawg answered so professionally and sincerely that had I not grown up in the projects, I would have been fooled. Hell, I almost believed his ass, and I knew the basis of the damn truth. I didn't know everything about the Murderville goon squad, but I knew damn well that Mad Dawg was not a security person only.

Listening to Michael Williams, you would have thought that Murder and his goons were some damn saints that attended church every Sunday and faithfully paid tithes. But fuck it! If that was his story, hopefully he stuck to it when we went to court, because the production he just put on in my office was exactly what I wanted on the stand during cross-examination. Bravo, Mr. Williams! Stellar performance.

I thought to myself, *one thug down, two more to go.* Everyone's testimony had to be on one accord 'cause one slip-up could lead to a lengthy sentence, and in my book, that was a loss. As far as I was concerned, losing in the courtroom was unacceptable. I soon drifted my attention back to my sister Co-Co and why she was on the witness list for the opposing team. Man, this shit was bothering the hell out of me.

An uneasiness soon began to settle in the pit of my stomach the more I thought about it. I made a mental note to talk with my sister sooner rather than later because surprises were what I did not want or need in defending this case. I knew I could get into some trouble by talking to a witness from the other side outside the trial, but she was my sister and who the fuck could prove that we weren't doing a little sisterly bonding? I believed I needed to know everything in order to defend my client properly. I could not wait any longer to talk to Co-Co, though, so I picked up my phone and dialed the last known number I had for the lil stripper girl. I hoped she answered and the conversation didn't end in a confrontation and cussing match.

Co-Co

"Ohh my god. What do this bourgeois bitch want with me?" I said after looking at my cell phone and noticing that it was Mikeela calling. The phone rang and rang because I decided not to answer. I shook my head, knowing that my sister dear was only calling about the case and she had probably found out about me being on the witness list for the prosecution. Kee-Kee was probably feeling some type of way about that, and so was I. I felt some type of way about Kee-Kee being the criminal attorney for Murderville, so frankly, my sister could just kiss my ass.

Damn! My phone was still ringing, so I finally answered the phone and held it to my ear. All I could hear was Kee-Kee screaming, "Hello?

Hello, Co-Co, Co-Co!" I didn't say a word. I just promptly ended the call. "Bitch," I said. I knew that Mikeela was in love with Murder. She had been since we were kids. Murder had Kee's nose wide open from jump street, but I planned to halt all this love shit and spill everything I knew about Murderville and his organization of goons up on the stand. I would deal with the consequences later, but Murderville needed to pay the piper for all the lives he had destroyed, including mine, my mother's, and sister's.

My granny used to always say that karma is a bitch, and she is always on time to deliver her brand of justice. I decided to let this situation rest for now because there was money to be made. I pulled up to the strip club, Club Body, got out of the car, and went in. As soon as I stepped through the door, I saw the manager, Davidson, and I rolled my eyes. I did not want to deal with this nasty ass man today. Luckily, he was busy with another chick named Candi Baby, and I was able to slide by without him noticing me.

It was Saturday, so I hoped the club would be packed and I would be able to make a nice bit of change tonight. I didn't know why, but the thought of making fast money got my coochie wet. I began to prepare for my show, and I planned to deliver a good one tonight because I had some stress to work off and some money to earn. I needed to figure out a way to make some extra money 'cause after I finished testifying in this damn case, I would probably have to skip town — that is, if I was alive long enough.

"Hey, Co-Co," Davidson said, interrupting my thoughts and my routine.

"What is it? Damn," I replied, "you scared the hell out of me! Do you know how to knock?" I did not allow him to say much.

"You are on in twenty minutes. We had a last-minute schedule change, so hurry the fuck up and get ready!" Davidson said and disappeared just as quickly as he had appeared.

"This dude!" I said to an empty room, shaking my head.

Black

The time had come for me to return to work after my four-day weekend. Today was now Monday, and I had to meet with the undercover team and report to that godforsaken prison job. I hated that damn place. I still couldn't believe that Officer Watkins was on the goon squad with Murderville and risking her freedom for some bullshit. But to each his own. To make matters worse, my sister was defending the motherfuckers I was trying to put away!

I was involved in this Murderville shit from all sides, and I hoped I didn't do anything to jeopardize accomplishing the goals that we had as an investigative unit. Another thing I had on my mind was my sister Co-Co calling for God knows what, but I was sure it had something to do with Murderville or some other criminal activity. I could remember hearing back in the day from the streets that my sister Co-Co and Murder had some dealings with setting dudes up and robbing them. I wasn't sure on the particulars of the situation, but I knew some foul shit had taken place between the two. I knew that Co-Co wanted something major, because she always called when she needed somebody to bail her ass out of whatever she managed to get herself in.

My mind drifted back to my dream from last night. I was terrified that it would soon be more than a dream. I had allowed my life to become dominated by Murderville. I was so sick of hearing and speaking this thug's name. I didn't know what to do. I slammed my fist into the steering wheel of my Jeep and screamed into the atmosphere, "Murder, you going down!" One way or another, this shit has got to end.

Mikeela

Co-Co's phone rang and rang. "Damn bitch. Pick up the phone," I said just under a whisper. Finally, someone picked up the phone.

"Hello? Hello, Co-Co, Co-Co! I hear you breathing!" I yelled into the receiver. Dial tone.

"Oh no, she didn't! This hood rat hung up the phone in my face!" I said as I sat looking confused about what just happened.

After gathering my composure, I figured I would just pay the slut a visit if she wanted to act that way toward me and see what she'd do then when I was standing in her fucking face. I'd go to that nasty ass club where she was shaking her ass in because I knew she ain't missing no money or attention. I decided to get back to my business and deal with my lil ratchet ass sister in due time. I spoke into the speaker.

"Mrs. Wallace, can you please set up appointments for the rest of the people on my witness list? Umm, that would be Mr. Stephen Jay and Rick Nichols. You can make it at their earliest convenience, but please make sure they understand that sooner is better than later."

"Okay, Ms. Rye, I will set these appointments up for you, and also, while I have your attention, Mr. McWalters is requesting that you call him as soon as possible."

"Thank you, ma'am. I will certainly do that."

I wondered what the hell Murderville wanted

with me, but I was not ready to call him just yet. I still had some other things to get done around the office, and that nigga was just a distraction to me and my horny ass. All I seemed to think about when he was on the phone or in the vicinity was getting it in. I had, for some reason, began to get nervous about my chances of actually winning this case for Murderville. It was indeed going to be a difficult task to accomplish. However, it was something I was willing to continue pursuing, and you could be damn sure I was willing to do whatever it took to have Murder free and in my bed full-time.

Co-Co

I had been having a rough week. For one, my money was looking funny from the club. Now, don't get me wrong, I was still making money, but it just wasn't the bank I had grown used to in the past weeks. Plus, to top shit off, this Murderville trial was lingering over my damn head. I was scheduled to testify for the State and run the chance of being labeled a snitch in the hood. I had been in this neighborhood my whole life, and I was sure that it would not be taken lightly my being a witness against the hood legend Murder. The old saying that snitches get stitches was swirling around my head, and I was too damn cute for that shit to happen. On the cool, though, my gut instinct was to run away and hide, but I had two children to take into consideration. My mind was spinning, and my nerves had me on edge. My nerves were shot to hell!

I looked down at my hands, and they were shaking uncontrollably. This shit had me shook. The other day, I was sure that I would be cool testifying against Murderville and his organization because I hated these mother-fuckers. As of right now, though, I wasn't sure if I could go through with it. The price to pay for that seemed to be too high, but since I had been subpoenaed, the choice really had already been made for me. I was stuck between a rock and a hard place. I said out loud, "I gotta figure this shit out real soon before they find my ass floating in the river!"

I made a mental note to reach out to my sisters, Black and Kee-Kee, before I made a final decision about what I was going to do. I knew one thing for sure, and that was that time was running out on my ass. I needed to figure out a plan ASAP because once Murderville found out that I was on a witness list for the other side, I was positive a bounty would be put on my head.

Black

I had just finished my shift and was headed out the door when I caught Watkins hemmed up in the corner with an inmate. From where I was standing at that moment, Officer Watkins could not see me. So I decided to move closer and position myself in a way that I could hear some of the conversation that seemed to be taking place between the two. The conversation seemed to be intense. I decided to maneuver myself in the side corner where Watkins and the inmate were, and to my surprise, I could hear them very well. The two carried on and were so into their exchange and were none the wiser to my presence. I listened intently, looking for information that would be beneficial to the case.

I heard Watkins say, "Hey, man, I'ma need for you to do whatever you need to do to move that weight through this prison faster than what you are. I'ma need for yo ass to make sure that yo peeps have the money in the spot so the boss can pick it up at the designated time. Lastly, I'ma need you to make sure no one comes up short on their payments or products, or it will most definitely come out yo ass." The inmate simply said, "Aight, I got cha, baby girl."

"Damn," was all I could manage to say. I was thinking that I wished I had a recorder or some way to get this bitch on tape to put her ass away for a long time. I didn't recognize the inmate right off, but I made a mental note to identify his ass as soon as possible. I could say that he seemed familiar. I was sure that I had seen his ass somewhere before. But where? I could not put my finger on it, and it was irritating the hell out of me.

I walked out of the facility, shaking my head, thinking it was a cold world and you could not trust anyone. In this game nowadays, everybody's looking to come up and don't mind shitting on the next person to get there.

Mikeela

I was sitting in my office, reviewing my case notes, and this was the first time in my nine years of practicing law that I felt nervous. I had built a reputation of being calm, cool, and collected. I was no holds barred, and I always came out the courtroom scoring a victory for my clients. I could not put my finger on it just yet, but there remained an uneasiness in the pit of my stomach. My intuition was telling me to run like hell away from this case 'cause something was not right and the shit was most likely gonna hit the fan.

I was contemplating the fact that maybe I should remove myself from counsel to Samuel while it was still early enough for him to obtain someone else to represent him. I thought that maybe I would run the idea by my client later and see how he'd feel about it.

I soon shook those thoughts from my head

and returned to gathering my notes on the last open case that I was defending before Murderville's case came on the docket. This current DWI case I had before me was a piece of cake compared to the biggest trial that Millville was about to showcase against Samuel McWalters. It was billed to be a showdown and had been sensationalized in the media. At that moment, my office door swung open and hit the wall with so much force that I could have sworn the building shook. I jumped from my seat, saying,

"What the hell!"

There in my office doorway stood Murderville, seething with anger and huffing and puffing. And before I could say another word, he yelled at the top of his damn lungs, "Bitch, when I call, you answer! I don't leave messages. This thing we got going on is serious business. My money and my life are on the line, and I will not be put on hold or ignored! Do you understand me?"

Needless to say, I was shocked. I had a lot going on in my head, but for some reason, nothing would come out of my mouth. That was probably for the best. I tell you I could literally not move or speak. Actually, I felt like I was going to shit myself. This nigga had me that scared, but in a strange way, I was equally aroused by the scene taking place in my office at the moment. Oh, my vagina was wet.

However, those thoughts soon left because I looked at Murderville's face for the first time since he had entered my office he-man style and, for the first time, I saw pure evil. I saw the man that everyone feared on the streets of Millville. It was in this moment that I feared for my life for the very first time. This motherfucker right here was crazy as hell, and I had better tread lightly. In my mind I was thinking, *What the fuck have I done? Shit just got real, and I have made a deal with the devil!*

Co-Co

I had bypassed going to work at the club for the past three days. I knew that Davidson's corny ass would be knocking on my door down soon. Did I mention I had been ignoring his phone calls and text messages as well? I knew Davidson was my boss, but fuck him and fuck that job right now! I had a lot of shit going on. I just could not get myself together enough to get out of bed.

Yes, I had been in bed for three damn days, stressing about this trial and Murderville bullshit. It was really getting the best of me and fucking up my frame of mind to the point that I was unable to function productively. To say the least, my nerves were rattled and I was on edge. I had sent my children, Ray-Ray and Juju, to live with relatives down in Paris, Texas. At least I did not have to worry about their safety if things around here started to get crazy. The fact that Murder and his goons were involved almost guaranteed that it would soon become hazardous to my health. I had considered joining my children once this current situation was over and done. But for now, I needed to come up with a plan that would ensure that once the smoke cleared, I would still be alive and well and Murderville and his gang would be where they belonged: six feet under or in prison for the rest of their natural lives.

I knew I needed to contact my sisters to gauge their knowledge of the trial situation. I wanted to see if Black had any helpful information since she was connected to the law enforcement community. I most definitely wanted to talk with Kee-Kee's ole high maintenance ass to see if she was defending her client, sexing him, or both.

Quiet as it was kept, I knew Kee-Kee was a hoe. The bitch was just on the down low with her shit and looking down on those of us who lived more openly. Yeah, I was about to shine the light on everybody's ass, 'cause if this was my last rodeo, I'm a clown on their asses. Straight like that. But in real life, I wanted to survive this situation. In order for that to happen, I just gotta be smart so I could walk away with a lot of cash and my life to get back with my children.

Black

I had decided to just come right out and ask Officer Watkins who the hell that inmate I saw her talking with was. I also wanted to know why they were cornered off away from everyone, engaged in an intense conversation. What possibly could an officer and an inmate have to speak with on a personal level?

Of course, I had heard the majority of the conversation and I knew the bitch was gonna lie, but confrontation was the method I had chosen to use. Frankly, this broad was getting on my last nerve. I decided to go for a run tonight to help clear my head and mull over some things. It seemed that everything was beginning to run together. The more I became engrossed in this undercover bullshit, the more my personal and professional lives were overlapping. I knew that eventually I would have to make some hard decisions. I just hoped that I would be able to live with the decisions and that my family would be left intact. I knew my sisters and I were not close, but blood was the tie that bound us together and made us family. Hopefully, my undercover work would eventually pay off and lead to a damn promotion and some recognition around this damn town.

Kee-Kee

I regained my composure, and as professionally as possible, I addressed Mr. Samuel McWalters. "Why in the world would you have the nerve and audacity to come in my place of business and act a damn fool? I am well aware of what the ramifications that go along with a case such as this are. However, you are not my boss, my father, or even my man. You're my friend, or my client, and with that being said, you are not even my only client."

I made my way from around my desk to the door and tried to close it to make the conversation between the two of us more private, but the damn door was off the hinge. I was so pissed, but the only thing I could do was shake my head. This motherfucker had lost his mind for real.

"This nigga's getting on my damn nerves," I mumbled from frustration, hoping that Murderville didn't hear me.

"What the fuck did you say?" he managed to say through clenched teeth.

Fuck it! I guessed it was too late and he did hear what I said, but oh well.

"What the hell is wrong with you, nigga? You cannot come in here like I'm one of your hoes on the street and you running something," I said.

"But you are one of my hoes! You have been since the projects. So is your mama and your sister. So stay in your lane and know your place, bitch. I run this, and if I call, whatever the time, you answer!" Murderville said. I could not believe my ears, and this was the man I had been contemplating spending my life with.

"Look, look," I began, "let's just calm down and start this conversation over."

"Fuck that! You are my lawyer. Therefore, you are working for me and what I say goes," he said.

"When I call, you answer. When I say jump, you need to say how high. I need to know what is going on with my case, and you putting me on hold or not returning my calls is not an option that you have," Murder continued. "Like I said in the beginning, I am your most important client and, as far as I am concerned, your only client. So you need to clear your schedule so that I am your top priority."

After all that, this nigga just turned and exited my office.

"Lawd, have mercy," I said. I was thankful I didn't have any other clients present in my office at that time. Danita Wallace, my secretary, appeared at the door.

"Are you okay, Ms. Rye?" she asked. I was still in somewhat of a daze, but I managed to answer.

"Yes, I am fine, but can you arrange for someone to come fix my door that hoodlum just pulled off the hinge?"

I plopped down in my office chair, confused and hurt. *What the hell have I gotten myself into? Lawd, you gotta be careful what you ask for because you just may get it.* I had asked for a high-profile case, and I got just that along with a hood nigga and some bullshit.

Co-Co

I had not decided on exactly how I was going to execute my plan on getting my revenge on Murderville, but I knew it had to be precise in order for me to walk away in one piece. I figured that somewhere in his organization of goons, there was one person secretly wanting to be in his place. There was always a hater and a snitch thirsty for the boss's status. I knew that where there was a hater, there was a person I needed to be an ally with.

I heard through the grapevine that one of Murder's associates was in lockup on a charge that he took for Murder. I had also learned that he was a snitch. Well, I knew he was an undercover snitch from his days in the projects. This nigga couldn't hold water. That was why I was surprised that Murder was even dealing with the dude. The dude's name was Beachie. Although nothing was for sure, I made up my mind to get a visit with this slime ass nigga to see what was good and where his loyalty really lies. I knew Beachie's sister Rene lived in the projects, in the building adjacent to mine. So after work, I planned to pay his sister a visit. Rene was hooked on drugs, so I figured that getting information from her would be easy. All I had to do was offer a little money, and Rene would probably tell me everything I wanted to know.

I hurried to the dressing room so that I could get ready to perform my set and get the hell out of the club. I wanted to catch Rene before she was lost in the streets for the next few days on her drug binge or doing whatever crackheads did for days at a time. I headed to Davidson's office to see if he would change the rotation of dancers around to accommodate me. I wanted to dance first tonight. This would enable me to get out early enough to catch Rene.

I approached Davidson's office and noticed the door was closed, which was strange because his door was rarely closed. I put my ear to the door. I couldn't hear anything, so I knocked. I then heard some commotion going on the other side. I knocked again, but louder. I then turned the knob, and the door swung open.

From where I was standing, I could see in Davidson's office clearly. I saw my mother, Earlene, giving this grimy old man some lip service. "Ohh my god!" I screamed at the top of my lungs.

The other girls ran out the dressing area to look at the scene I was creating. I didn't give two fucks. I was about to clown. Davidson, by this time, had jumped up, dick in hand, saying, "Why, why, why you ain't k-k-k-knockin' on the damn doe, Co-Co?"

My mother just stood there with the dumbest look on her face. I walked over to my mother and punched her in the face with a closed fist. This bitch knew I worked here. Why did she bring this shit here with his motherfucker? I was so embarrassed. Davidson jumped between the two of us before I could complete my second attempt to punch my mother. I wanted to drag her through the club. I knew she was my mother, but I was so sick and tired of this selfish bitch only thinking about her needs.

Yes, I was grown, but the child that she never nurtured still resided in me. I continued to hope for once in this lifetime that I could have a mother-daughter moment. I snapped out of my trance to Davidson saying, "That i-i-is still your . . . your mother, g-g-girl, have some respect," I could not deal with this stuttering ass nigga right now. The shit was pissing me off. "Yeah? Like you was respecting her by having her on her knees in a place where I work!" I screamed back at Davidson. "You know what? Fuck you, her, and this whole damn place! I ain't working in this motherfucker tonight. Now, respect that," I said.

I then turned and stormed out of the office into the hallway. "Okay, you dumb, thirsty ass bitches, the show is over! Carry on!" I yelled at the other strippers that had gathered in the hallway to be nosy. I then turned and stormed out the club. I loved my mother as best I could, but I just could not forget or forgive the shit she continued to do. I left the club and ran to my car with tears streaming down my face. I knew I would never escape the sins of my mother unless I left Millville forever. In all the years my mother was on the streets, I had never actually seen her in action with a man. Of course, my mother was grown, but having the image of my mother with a random dick in her mouth was still a fucked up picture to have replaying in my head. "Damn," was all I had the strength to say.

Black

As I prepared for my shift at the prison

tonight, I went over my plan to confront Officer Watkins about the nature of the relationship between her and the inmate. I had just decided to confront her with what I had seen, not about the conversation I overheard. I would save that for a later date. I guess what I was struggling with was how to approach her. *Do I go aggressive in my questioning, or do I go nice and carefree?* You know what? I believed I would just go up and ask her straight up and see what happened. Being real was all I knew. *So why change now?* It was not like this female could whip my ass or something.

I had recently learned that the inmate's name was Beachie and he was an associate of Murderville. I tell you what, this Murderville had his hands in everything criminally related. I also learned that Beachie's real name was John Sims. The rumor on the street was that Beachie was a damn informant and he was vying to take Murder's place once he was convicted. I wondered if I could find out some information about Beachie through my law enforcement connections. If in fact this man was indeed an informant, maybe I didn't really need to work so hard to find out what I needed to know about Officer Watkins and Murderville. I was sure he knew everything I wanted to make my case and end this undercover assignment because quite frankly, I was tired.

I left my house early so that if I happened to

see Watkins' dirty ass, I would have time to interrogate her. I pulled up in the parking lot, and out of my peripheral vision I saw Murderville's custom Mercedes SUV. I decided to park with my Jeep backed in so I could peep out the scene. I didn't have long to wait. Lo and behold, that bitch Watkins got out the passenger side, zipping up her uniform pants. Then she sashayed her ass around to the driver's side and delivered a passion-filled kiss, tongue and all. I assumed the driver was Murderville. I could only shake my head. This bitch right here had no integrity and no shame. Bitches like this could be very dangerous.

Mikeela

I had been trying to reach Murderville all damn day to discuss our altercation in my office, but the nigga would not pick up the phone. So I took it upon myself and drove by his little hangout. I had circled the place three times and saw his SUV outside. I just couldn't bring myself to go in.

Eventually, I decided to park and go in. As I was parking, Murder exited with some random bitch on his arm. I contemplated confronting him, but considering how he showed his ass previously, I decided to stay in my car. Now this bitch was all over my man. I gotta be honest, I was all up in my feelings. After kissing with tongue involved, these two got in his Mercedes and sped off. They were so engrossed in touching and kissing that Murderville didn't even notice me or my car in plain view. So I decided like a thirsty ass female to follow them and see where they were going. After thirty minutes of following these fools, I ended up in front of the Millville prison, where my sister Black was reportedly working.

I hadn't talked to my sister in a while, a fact that I was not proud of, but it was what it was. The female in the car with Murder stepped out the car from the passenger side in a correctional officer's uniform, so I assumed she must have changed in the damn car. The bitch wasn't wearing that shit when she and Murder exited his after-hours spot. Then she went around to the driver's side and put her tongue in my man's mouth. Damn! My blood was boiling hot. I must admit, I was jealous and all kinds of hurt. I couldn't take any more, so I put my car in drive and drove off, feeling some type of way about a man that I had spent my whole life loving.

Co-Co

I was still in a different headspace after what happened at the club last night. I didn't even go find Beachie's sister, Rene, to get the scoop on him. No matter the age of the child, it does something to the soul to walk in and see your mother with a random dick in her mouth—a dirty ass man at that—in the office of a strip club. I knew I couldn't allow for last night's drama to sidetrack my planned agenda. *Let me get out this bed and get dressed to go and see if Rene is at her house.* I wanted her to tell her brother that I needed to speak with him and to put me on his visitation list.

I planned to go visit Beachie and shoot the breeze about old times to gauge his attitude toward Murderville. I wanted to test his loyalty and see how open this nigga was about spilling inside information about the organization. I knew that back in the day, Beachie and Murder had some beef because Murder had turned his sister Rene out. In Murderville fashion, he then put Rene out on the street to trick for him, of course. The rumor was that Beachie and Murder had recently got collared together while out trying to make a drop. Beachie ended up saying that the drugs and shit in the car were all his and that Murder had no knowledge of what was going on. With it being Beachie's car and him making a damn jailhouse confession, taking the rap, the authorities had no choice but to let Murder go again.

Although Beachie had taken the rap for Murder, Murder had not been to see him or check on his family. Nor had that nigga provided any financial assistance to Beachie or his family, as was the norm when a motherfucker took a charge for your ass. This had not been the first time that Beachie had done something like this to save Murder's ass either. I guessed his dumb ass would learn one day. Maybe that was why the nigga turned to snitching to get payback. In any event, I didn't give a fuck what they had going on. I was hoping that Beachie would sing like a bird and give me what I needed to use to benefit my agenda.

Damn, I couldn't help but think that you gotta respect the game but the game ain't got no respect for no one. I hoped this bitch was home, 'cause I only wanted to visit her one time. Though I lived in the projects, I didn't hang out often. I had done enough of that in my younger years, and it hadn't benefited me any then. I just went to work and stayed closed up in my little-ass apartment, wishing soon I could leave this shit behind. I arrived at Rene's apartment and knocked on the door. No answer. I knocked again. Still no answer. I then turned the knob, and the door crept open. I pushed on the door as slowly as possible 'cause I didn't want to be surprised by anything.

"Hello, heello, hello, Rene? Rene!" I yelled. Still no answer. I was standing in the front room of the apartment, and from where I was, it seemed as though no one was in the trashed out place.

"Damn, her apartment is nasty as hell!" I said

out loud. I thought I heard movement in the back. I screamed Rene's name again. Then I heard moaning and sex sounds coming from the back room.

"Oohh, oohh, yesss, ummm!"

I assumed the hoe was turning a trick at seven o'clock in the morning. A twenty-four-hour, seven day a week hoe. I could not do anything but stand and wait. I'd be damned if I sat anywhere in this nasty apartment. I was on a mission. This conversation needed to be had today, and that was the only reason I had chosen to wait until Rene surfaced from the back room.

Black

I was watching the show Watkins and Murder had been putting on for about twenty minutes now. I was tired of looking, so I decided to go over and interrupt. By the time I had made it up to the Mercedes, Watkins was done and making herself presentable.

"Hey, Watkins," I said, walking up on her like I didn't just see what had occurred between her and Murder or like I didn't see this tricked out Mercedes sticking out like a sore thumb. Watkins was shocked and looked embarrassed. I kinda laughed to myself because I didn't think Watkins had any tact about anything she did. Honestly, the shit was hilarious as hell to me.

"Hey, Murderville, what's good?" I said.

"What it do, Black?" this motherfucker replied to me like we were cool.

The sound of his voice made my skin crawl.

"I'm good. Y'all was out here getting it in. I enjoyed the show. Tell my sister Kee-Kee I said what's up," I said while staring Watkins down. After the little exchange with Murder, I turned to walk toward the entrance of the facility because in that moment, I had become really irritated with the presence of this thug and this hoe. Watkins soon caught up with my stride, and as we entered the facility doors, I asked,

"So, Watkins, you hoeing now?"

She just looked at me and rolled her eyes. Then she said "Whatever, hata" and some other shit I couldn't quite understand. She entered the women's restroom, I assumed, to clean up a bit. I had to get my head right if I was gonna approach Watkins and get information from her ass. I had almost reached the entrance of the briefing room when I heard Officer Watkins calling my name. I didn't even bother turning around. I just stood there and waited until she caught up with me.

"What the fuck was those little comments about outside, bitch? Was you trying to be funny? 'Cause it ain't no shame in my game." Watkins said all in one damn breath.

"Obviously," I replied, "but fuck that, 'cause everybody know you a hoe and Murderville a hoe, so why sweat it?" I threw in a fake laugh to try to lighten the mood. I wanted to change the subject, so I said,

"Watkins, who was that inmate I saw you talking to cornered off on zone 1 yesterday?"

At first, she tried to pretend like she had no idea what I was talking about. I continued to push the subject with her because I wanted to get all the information I could while she was still speaking to me. This bitch was talking with the enemy, and she didn't even know it. A lot of times, the love of money and attention can lead you into some compromising situations. That's why you gotta live and choose wisely.

Mikeela

After I had seen Murderville leave with that bitch riding his nuts like she was his girl, I was definitely feeling some type of way. My personal and professional feelings had certainly intertwined. I needed to check myself before shit got too real. I needed to reevaluate the situation I was currently in and put my feelings in check. Fuck losing my career and my lifestyle for the love of a nigga! Hell, I was living too damn good to be that stupid.

However, I was a woman and I did appreciate how Murder served that dick. I did love that man, and seeing him be the womanizer I knew he was still stung like hell. Considering how that bastard acted the last time he was in my office; I knew I needed to tread lightly when dealing with him from now on. I also knew I would most definitely not be sexing the nigga anytime soon. I felt that he could probably still talk my ass out my panties, but the resolution sounded good in my head. For now, though, when dealing with Murder, I would just be professional until I could figure out how to deal this nigga a dose of his own medicine.

I was shaking my head and wondering at the same time when the hell I would quit trying to offer my love to street niggas. *You can take the girl out of the hood, but you cannot take the hood out of the girl.* Despite my leaving the projects so long ago and despite my profession, I was still straight ratchet.

Co-Co

I stood in the living room of this nasty place for what seemed like an eternity. But in actuality, it was more like thirty minutes. Rene finally came stumbling out, and I could tell she was high as hell. Her eyes were damn near closed. I wasn't sure if she was awake or sleepwalking. I called her name again anyway.

"Rene, Rene," I yelled.

She replied, "Wait a minute, bitch. And who the hell let you in my damn apartment? Who the fuck is you anyway?"

I chuckled to keep from getting mad, and I let her make it since I really needed her on my team at the moment. Just then, some random nigga from around the way came bopping his ass to the front room, fixing his clothes and shit. When he looked up and recognized who I was, I saw pure embarrassment on his face. I looked his ass straight in the face to make sure he knew I saw him, and if he wanted to act a fool in the future, I would most definitely clown that ass. He was one of those low-budget dudes that would be talking shit about crackheads and prostitutes on the block, but when nobody was looking, he'd be breaking bread with them and sexing them. Hell, he must be in love with that glass pipe his damn self. Ole nasty ass. After lil nasty left, I turned my attention to Rene, and by this time, she was on her sofa, asleep. I was frustrated by this time and went over to her and started shaking her really hard to wake her up. After about five minutes, she finally woke up.

"Damn, Rene, what the hell is wrong with you? You need to stop smoking them damn drugs and shit. And you need to clean up this nasty-ass apartment. What type of woman lives like this?" I told her as calmly as I could manage.

"Yo mama bitch!" Rene replied.

I had to admit that comment stung 'cause it was true. I found myself in my feelings about to choke this hoe out, so I just silently counted to ten.

"Okay, Rene check this; I ain't got time for your crackhead comments, antics, or games. I need for you to contact that brother of yours, Beachie, and get him to add me to his visitation list. You already know my name is Co-Co Rye, and he will know me too once you mention my name," I said to her.

"And what if I don't?" she countered.

"I'ma beat that ass," I said as I turned and walked out the crackhead's apartment.

Black

Watkins had told me that she and the inmate were talking about some jail business and some other bullshit she had thrown in the mix. I couldn't do nothing but laugh. On my own I found out that the inmate's name was Beachie, one of Murderville's goons. He had landed in prison after being jammed up on a drug charge after the cops searched the car that he and Murder were riding. Now that I had that information, I needed to find out who else was involved in the drug enterprise inside Millville State Prison. I believed that Watkins was the inside connect, and the conversation that I had overheard told me that this Beachie character was involved as well. I could not believe that Officer Bre Watkins would risk her career and her freedom for a man. Some people were just that stupid and thirsty.

I haven't quite figured out how to go about getting the information that I needed for the sake of my undercover assignment without tipping people off. I did know that the inmates would practically sell their souls for commissary, so I just needed to find somebody that was hungry and ready to snitch. I would pay attention to my surroundings, and eventually I know that the right snitches would make themselves known. I had so many questions going on in my head, and I needed to obtain the answers to them all. I wanted to know the extent of Watkins's involvement with Murderville, and what kind of drug enterprise was in full effect. I mean, I knew Watkins and Murder were fucking, but would that constitute a person to risk everything they had going for them? Really? As soon as I gained all the needed information, I was going to bust that bitch and anyone else connected to her operation.

Mikeela

So I said that I would only deal with Murder on a professional level, but my feelings and the yearning between my legs were definitely telling me that was a lie. I was yearning for his touch and for him to take me to an extreme orgasm. I knew that I needed to put myself in check, but that was easier said than done. I was a sad case 'cause I still wanted him despite the fact of my seeing him with another bitch. My body wanted what my body wanted, and I was inclined to surrender to its desires. Murderville was on the way to my office so that we could have a discussion to hash out our differences. I wanted this conversation to go in a positive direction so that we could get our relationship back on track. Our focus needed to be totally on winning the case and maintaining his freedom. Sex on the side would be good as well. My intercom buzzed and snapped me back to the reality of my current situation.

"Yes, Mrs. Wallace," I said into the intercom.

"Mr. McWalters is here to see you," she replied.

"Send him in," I said.

This man's intoxicating cologne entered my office before he did, and I promise I tried to put on my best professional face. However, when I made eye contact, all that professional shit went out the window. I was mesmerized, in love, and in lust all over again. I wanted to sex his sexy ass right there and right then. The desire was so strong, so I got up and sashayed over and closed and locked my office door.

I then walked up to Mr. McWalters and proceeded to undress him from the waist down. I tongued him down and forcefully pushed him down in the corner chair in my office. I lowered myself onto his erect package and began to ride off into the land of ecstasy. When I had finished after round 2, I excused myself to my bathroom to freshen up.

I returned to my office to find Murder looking through my files and other things on my desk.

"Excuse me, can I help you with something?" I said, slightly offended.

"I'm looking for the witness list for the prosecution because I heard that your hoe of sista, Co-Co, was on that motherfucker," Murder responded.

I knew that Co-Co was on the list, but I hadn't told him for reasons I didn't quite understand yet. I wasn't about to tell him shit right now, so I lied. "I haven't gotten around to obtaining a witness list from the prosecution yet. I'm still focused on our witnesses by making sure that their stories are on one accord." Murder looked at me like he knew I was full of shit, but he left the subject alone, at least for the time being. I knew it was about to get real, and I needed to immediately see what the hell my sister had to do with this Murderville street life. How was this situation going to affect my case and my life? I began to worry about my decision to get involved with this bullshit in the first place, but one thing was for certain if push came to shove, I would not be the one holding the short end of the stick on this deal. And you could take that to the bank!

Co-Co

Rene had shown up at Club Body to let me know that Beachie was cool with putting me on his visitation list. So, I was trying to figure out how to approach him about his business with Murder. I had a little street knowledge, but I was not a pro. I knew most dudes thought I was fine and sexy, so I figured that Beachie was still on that level too. After all, he was still a man and they usually got caught thinking with the wrong head. I planned to use his dumb ass to my advantage. I started going through my closet like a mad woman, trying to see if I could find the sexiest outfit to get this nigga's attention and fuck up his mind on my very first visit. They say the first impression is the most important, and I planned to make mine memorable. When it came to dealing with me, I wanted Beachie to think sex.

Once I had him on my team, I planned to keep him and use him until I got what I needed. By the time he figured out what was up, I planned to be gone with the wind. I had to get Beachie to fall in love hard and fast 'cause that would make getting information that much easier. Luckily, he was locked up, so I didn't have to physically sleep with his ugly ass. I just had to play with his mind so good that he wouldn't miss the physical contact. I knew that MD would be coming to me soon about meeting Murderville, so because of that fact, I was on borrowed time. I needed to get Beachie's snitching ass talking fast to help formulate a plan before it was time for my ass to pay the piper.

Black

I had not quite figured out how deep this drug shit was at Millville State Prison, but I assumed that when it was all said and done, heads were gonna shake and eyes would be rolling. Watkins had built a stellar career of about fifteen years of service, and I couldn't fathom why she would risk that along with her freedom. The shit was just dumb as hell to me, but to each his own. Maybe the dick that Murderville was serving her was just that good. So good that it would make a bitch forget her common sense. The thought was amazing to me because I would never allow a man to control me like that—*never*! I had been off work for the past few days, and I was enjoying that shit. I was chillaxin'.

I thought about returning Co-Co's phone call, but hell, I wasn't ready for her ass either. I loved my sisters, I really did, but I just couldn't stand their asses most of the time. Co-Co had become the project hoe, and Kee-Kee thought her shit didn't stink. Once I left the Millville projects, I just felt that I needed to shut everything tied to that life out. I never meant for so much time to pass without contacting my family. I had to do what was best for Black at that time. I would eventually call Co-Co, but today was not going to be the day. Instead of drama, I was going to put in a movie and continue to chill. Today I would not be thinking about work, Watkins, Murder, or my sisters. Yes, today I was going to be in chill mode all day.

Mikeela

I decided not to go into the office for the second day in a row. I was feeling some type of way. I felt safer at home, so I just worked on Murderville's case from my house. I probably should have just excused myself from this damn case since I was so close to the major players. My pride would not let me do it. My mother had once told me that my pride would be the cause of my demise, but I dismissed anything that bitch said. She was in love with the streets and a crackhead, so what the hell did she know?

I picked up the phone to call Co-Co again, and hopefully, the little stripper would answer. The phone rang once, twice, and on the third time, I heard her voice. "Hello? Heellooo!" But I froze. It had been at least five years since I had heard my sister's voice. For some reason, I was emotional and I teared up. Man, I was messed up. I never knew how much I missed my sister until that very moment.

"Okay, who the hell is this playing on my damn phone? Hello! Hello!" Co-Co was saying. I finally gathered my composure and said, "Hey, Co-Co, it's your sister Kee-Kee."

She replied, "Oh, now I'm yo sister. You claiming me now?"

"Hello again, hunty. How are you? How have you been?" I said trying to ignore her question and her attitude.

"I'm good. What is it you want?" Co-Co said, attitude still intact. I said, "How you know I want something?"

"It's been five years at least since I heard from the high and mighty attorney at law. Again, I ask, what the fuck you want with me, sister dear?" was her reply.

"Okay, fine. What business do you have with Murderville, and how does it affect my case?" I said to her.

I then heard nothing from the other end of the damn phone. This bitch hung up the phone in my damn face again and without answering my question. I knew I wasn't supposed to be calling and asking Co-Co shit about the case and her testimony. Whatever! I needed to know why the prosecution felt that she was significant enough to put on their witness list. Co-Co had avoided me this time, but I promised next time, the outcome would be different.

Shit, I was hoping her dumb ass didn't know that. Even if she did, I trusted that she wouldn't turn me in. At least I hoped so.

Co-Co

I had seen the caller ID that it was my sister Kee-Kee calling my phone again. I hadn't heard from her ass in at least five years, so I knew she wasn't calling to check on my well-being. I started not to answer, but on the third ring, I picked up the call. There was a little part of me that wanted to hear her voice again.

"Hello, heello," I said.

There was no answer, but I knew she was there 'cause I could hear her breathing. Damn, I was thinking to myself, *What is wrong with this bitch?*

Kee-Kee finally began to speak, and of course, she wanted to know about my connection with Murderville. My sister, concerned about her case and her nigga, in total disregard to my feelings or my safety. I didn't want to talk to her ass once she asked the damn question about being involved with Murder. She was working with the enemy, so yes, I introduced her ass to the dial tone. Dismissed. I was pissed off all over again. The idea that Kee-Kee would defend that motherfucker Murderville enraged me. All my life, Kee-Kee and my mom, Earlene, had always chosen a man over family. Where was the fucking loyalty to your blood? I was the youngest, and all their asses had left me to do for myself. If nobody wanted to stand up for Co-Co, then I would start standing for myself. Right here and right now. Fuck Mikeela and fuck Murderville! Fuck everybody, for that matter. Trust nobody but God.

Black

Well, today was a new day, and my ass had to return to the grind. I hurriedly readied myself for work and rushed to my Jeep. I didn't know why I was in such a rush to go to the prison. This shit rarely happened. I hated this undercover stint I was doing, but hopefully, when it was all said and done, the community of Millville would be sitting in a better place.

I knew that arresting Murderville would not end our city's drug problem, because for every drug ring that's ended, one is waiting in the wings to take its position. However, this particular case right here would be beneficial to me and my own personal interests. I pulled up to work, and since I was at least an hour early, I decided to go and wait for briefing in our designated break room.

On my way to the break room, I heard what sounded like moaning noises on the back end of the prison building. This was the area where foot traffic was slim to none. At first, I thought that my mind was playing tricks on me. I stopped in my tracks and was thinking, *Surely, no one would be sexing in a monitored jail facility.*

I then heard the sound again, so I put my ear

to where the sounds were coming from. Lo and behold, I heard this moaning and shit again. I didn't know what to do because I was both excited and amazed. So I just stood there looking like a damn fool 'cause I wanted to know who was brave enough to be fucking in a jail facility. There were no cameras focused on this particular part of the jail because it was in a no-traffic zone. This meant that in transporting inmates, this area was supposed to be restricted from passing through. I posted up for about thirty minutes. Damn, my adrenaline was pumping. I was definitely determined to see this shit play out, and I was definitely ready to blast whoever's ass was in this damn nasty ass maintenance area having sex.

Finally, the door opened, and my ass almost passed out from the anticipation. Guess who came sashaying out? Watkins. Well, I'd be damned! It was indeed Officer Watkins and Beachie. This nasty bitch is having sex with an inmate on the clock and in the jail facility. To be honest, this shit didn't surprise me, and the look on her face was priceless.

I said, "Watkins, what the fuck are you doing? Were you in there having relations with a damn inmate?" I was laughing on the inside, but on the outside, I was trying to maintain a serious, professional demeanor.

Watkins simply said, "Mind yo bizness and you will be safe!"

I knew this bitch didn't just have the audacity to threaten me. She was definitely feeling herself, and I couldn't wait to deal her a dose of reality, because for every action and decision, there is always a reaction and consequences that one has to deal with.

"What the hell is that supposed to mean?" I yelled after her.

"Mind your motherfucking bizness," she said with emphasis on her words, and then she walked off like she was Ms. America or somebody.

"Say, you ole nasty bitch, I know you did not just threaten me and walk the fuck off like you the shit. I am not afraid of your ass or anybody else walking around here!" I screamed back at her.

She shot me the finger and continued walking off with the inmate in tow. I didn't know what to do, but I did know that shit at this prison was out of control. I was hoping that soon it would be over, and that Watkins hadn't fucked everybody in here by that time. Damn, a hoe's gonna always be a hoe.

Mikeela

I was kinda hurt and in my feelings about how the conversation that I had with Co-Co went. After all, she was my lil sister, my blood. I knew that leaving her behind in the Millville projects might have affected her, but hell, I was not her mother. It wasn't like I left her alone. Black was there, and I figured they would be there for each other. Eventually, though, Black's ass left too. I was hurting, and in order for me to live a better life, I had to run when I did. It was a selfish move, maybe, but I needed to heal in order to survive. Hopefully soon, we all could come together and make amends. Truth be told, I missed the sisterly bond that we once shared trying to survive in the projects.

For the past few days, I had been working from the house, collecting files and information that I was going to use in my defense case. I had lined up some of the local charity supervisors to be character witnesses for Murderville to show his involvement in the community on a positive level. I also planned to discredit the witnesses on the prosecution's list by bringing into light some of the misdeeds that they had committed against the society as well. The majority of the people on that damn list were also career criminals. I was hoping that someway, somehow, the trial would end in a mistrial. At least that way, my job would be done and the professional relationship between Murderville and I would be done and over.

I had heard about this Beachie character who had just recently been arrested. The word on the street was, it had something to do with Murderville. I knew Beachie was high up on the rankings in Murderville's organization, however, what he did exactly, I wasn't sure. I knew the shit was illegal, so maybe it was good that I did not know the ins and outs of the organization. I hadn't seen Beachie's name on any witness list yet, so I wanted to go to the Millville State Prison and question his ass. I was curious to see how loyal he was to his boss and see where his thought process was if he became a witness. Rumor had it that Beachie was a snitch and working for the feds, but I needed to try everything and everybody to accomplish my goals of winning this damn case.

I was getting cabin fever, so I arranged for my secretary and my two paralegals to meet me at the local fast food joint for some wings. I really just didn't want to be in the restaurant solo and would like to use this time to discuss the case strategy with my team as well. I arrived at the restaurant a little early to get us a good table. I always situated myself to be facing the door. I never wanted something to go down and not be prepared for it because my back was facing the door. I needed to be ready to run and take cover at all times, because people these days were too damn crazy.

Finally, everyone arrived and we placed our orders and waited. Sarah Smith, my senior paralegal, asked, "Ms. Rye, how do you feel about your chances of winning this case for Murderville?"

I reluctantly answered, "I am totally confident about our chances for victory. My track record and reputation will not let me believe any other way."

Our order eventually arrived, and everyone got situated and ready to eat. As I was about to bite into my lemon-pepper chicken wing, I overheard and saw some commotion going on in front of a big screen out of my peripheral vision. I turned toward the ruckus to see if we needed to vacate the premises or take cover. I looked up to the flat screen, and there was breaking news. The noise level had become ridiculous inside the restaurant, so I could only read the scrolling message at the bottom. It said, "Breaking news! Local attorney Sand White's body found after it washed ashore at around noon today." I was floored. I sure as hell hoped that Murderville didn't have shit to do with this man's murder. I almost shit in my pants because my instinct and experience told me that of course, my client was involved. After all, it was his MO. I immediately picked up my cell and dialed Murder's number. It went straight to voice mail. I wasn't only worried about whether Murder was involved. I was also worried if my ass was next. At this moment, I could literally shit bricks.

Co-Co

I had finally decided to go to Millville State Prison to visit Beachie's narc ass to see where his mind was regarding Murderville. I really didn't know what I planned to get from him or how he would help me carry out my plans to get revenge on his boss. I felt that it wouldn't hurt to go talk to him, and maybe I could get lucky.

I went to my closet and pulled out some tight skinny jeans that fit my ass like *pow*! I then selected a striped button-down shirt that I planned to tie up in the front and leave unbuttoned so my breasts could be in full view. I wanted Beachie to be so turned on by my body and looks that he would tell me whatever the hell I wanted to know. Beachie was the type of nigga that usually thought with the wrong head when he was dealing with a female. If you know what I mean. What was so sad was that he didn't care what the female looked like either. Fat, skinny, ugly, or beautiful, Beachie didn't give a fuck. He would sex anything with a vagina. I planned to use that to my advantage. Hell, I would even throw a little money on the nigga's books for commissary if he told me something good.

I was finally ready to head to the prison. I did a once over in the mirror. If I must say so myself, I was the shit and my body was the truth. This should be like taking candy from a baby. When I was done, this nigga wouldn't know what hit him. The bonus factor on this shit would be that I would get what I wanted and not even have to come off no pussy.

Black

I was sitting in my assigned zone, zone number 3, at the prison thinking about the incident I witnessed between Officer Watkins and the inmate Beachie. I was amazed. I just never would have figured that she would turn out to be involved in this drug ring inside the prison, and I would not have figured that she was such a whore. Some women these days are just so disrespectful to their bodies. I didn't know what I was gonna do with the new information at this point in the game. I had to be careful and make smart, precise decisions to accomplish the goal I wanted to accomplish.

"Code red" rang over the prison intercom, interrupting my thoughts. Since this particular code meant inmate altercation, I went around zone 2 to see if I could lend a hand. However, I did take my time reporting to the zone. I just wanted to make it seem as if I was there to lend a hand and not actually have to do anything. I was not in no damn hurry 'cause if the inmates wanted to try to kill one another, hell, my feeling was to let them.

When I finally arrived, I noticed that the situation had been handled by other officers. Interestingly enough, one of the inmates involved in the commotion was Beachie, and the other one was an inmate that went by the name of White Boy. You know, the ones that act and talk black until some shit goes down and they're somewhere in interrogation, snitching on everybody and their mama.

Now, just yesterday, these two fools were cool. I wondered if the sexcapade between Beachie and Watkins had something to do with this damn fight between these two.

Recently, White Boy had been in a verbal sparring with Officer Watkins, in which he was name calling and saying she sucked inmates' dicks and shit. Usually, when an inmate mouths off about stuff like that, officers don't pay attention because that is just inmate behavior. Considering what I had seen from Watkins's behavior, I needed to pay more attention to what the hell these inmates were saying 'cause the shit just might be the truth.

This Officer Watkins was one foul ass female, and she most definitely now got my undivided attention. If there was one thing I hated, it was a fake, foul ass officer, and I just added this bitch to my shit list. I was more than determined now than ever to bring her ass down too. Ole stank bitch!

Mikeela

I still had not been able to reach Murderville. I knew this motherfucker was avoiding my calls. I didn't have any time to deal with his games and bullshit, and I damn sure didn't have time to deal with extra bodies that just happened to float up and appear on dry land. Murder was already facing a slew of charges, and now his ex-lawyer/friend was dead. By the looks of the shit, the trail led back to his ass.

This nigga was starting to work my damn nerves. My heart was beating a mile a minute. I just felt that if I could just talk to Murder to see where his mindset was, I would feel a little better. This nigga would not answer his phone or return my text messages for shit. At this point, I missed my predictable cases and white-collar criminals. That shit was easy money and had no damn drama on my end, at least.

I headed to my car parked in the Buffalo Wild Wings parking lot, and out of the corner of my eye I could see a woman coming in my direction. She looked a little disheveled. I didn't recognize her, so I continued on my way to my car. I had enough shit to worry about already. I pushed my key to unlock my car.

As I reached for my car door, someone grabbed my arm, saying, "Hello, Mikeela."

I immediately snatched my arm away from their grasp and spun around with pepper spray, ready for action. However, when I turned around, I was looking into the face of my mother, Earlene Rye. The disheveled woman had been my mother, and I had not even recognized her. I was heartbroken at first glance, but then almost instantly, I became angry, embarrassed.

"Fucking crack whore!" I said. I angrily opened my car door and got in, started my car, and proceeded to leave. I looked in her direction one last time, and she looked a hot mess. I was still that girl searching for her mother, who had left so long ago.

My mother used to be a very beautiful woman with so much potential, but she fell victim to the streets. All I could see when I looked at her now was weakness, and I could not stand that shit.

I rolled down the driver's side window and threw a few bills out. She hurriedly went to pick the money off the ground. She was eager to get any crumbs from anybody. She didn't give a damn where it came from, and seeing her reaction to the money pissed me off even more. I sped the fuck off. I had no words for her, and I was still held captive by hurt and pain. I didn't think I could ever forgive a woman who chose to suck on a glass dick instead of being a mother to the children she had birthed into this world. This had turned out to be a very shitty day.

Co-Co

I finally made it to the Millville State Prison in about forty-five minutes. I had the pedal to the metal. I wanted to get there and get this shit over with.

I had known Beachie from around the way, but I never paid him any mind because he was wack and corny as hell. He would be hustling with Murda and 'em, but hell, it seemed like he never really came up like they did. Well, that was just my observation on the situation. I felt like if I were hustling with your ass, I needed to be eating like your ass was eating, or I would be moving around to some other shit that was more beneficial to me. Hell, if you were on a nigga team and you was putting in work, why you ain't making stacks like they was making? Maybe that was why Beachie's ass was snitching. He was salty about that money. Ha-ha, this shit was funny to me.

Nigga, you big mad or nah? I guess if you can't eat like they eating and stunt like they stuntin', hell start snitching on that ass. I don't agree with that logic, but to each his own.

I made it to the security gate and showed my ID and was cleared by top-notch security to go ahead and go through. I promise, these Kmart, wannabe cop motherfuckers got on my damn nerves. Really, they were taking their job to another level and were barely qualified for the job they got. Damn.

I finally got inside the building, and thank goodness, there was not a long ass line to sign in. I proceed to sign in with the ugly ass chick at the front desk. I told her I came to see John "Beachie" Sims, and took a seat. By the look on the bitch's face, I could tell she was dry ass hatin'. *Really, though, don't hate me, hate the game.*

As I was laughing to myself, I was thinking, *Hell, if I was that bitch, I would hate me too.* My clothes and shoe game stayed on fleek. After waiting for a damn hour, I sashayed back up to the reception area, making sure to make my ass hop, and asked the ugly chick, "Why the hell is it taking so damn long?"

She then said, "Ohh, my bad. Mr. Sims can't have any visits today. He is in isolation from an earlier altercation that occurred today."

I was pissed off 'cause this female knew that shit when she typed his damn name in the system to see where he was being housed. I started to cause a scene, but how my life was set up at that moment, I really needed to be free and not locked up. So, I snatched my ID and walked away. I had wasted a whole damn day in this drive up here to this place, and nothing happened. Damn, I needed to talk to this Beachie soon 'cause I knew my time was running out. Maybe I need to rethink my game plan and come up with a plan B.

I drove the rest of the way home in silence. No radio or nothing. I had shit on my mind, and I needed to think it all out.

Black

After things had calmed down from the code being called, I went to zone 4 to see if Watkins was around. I went around the corner, and there she was, standing between Officer Williams's damn legs, facing his chest, whispering in his ear. I just laughed really loud, trying to get her attention.

This bitch just looked at me like I wasn't shit and returned to whispering in Williams's ear. I said, "Damn, Watkins, it's like that? You ain't got no love for me no mo!"

Wouldn't you know, this ratchet ass female turned to me, stuck up her middle finger in my face, and sashayed off like she was right. At this point, she had gotten on my last damn nerve. It was past the time I checked this bitch. So I followed her around the corner, and as soon as I was close enough, I grabbed her arm and slammed that ass against the wall.

"Bitch, what the fuck is your problem?"

"You the one sexing that Beachie character, Murder, and God knows who else!"

"You ain't nothing but a two bit whore, and you don't get to disrespect me, 'cause I will dust that ass!" I said to Watkins while I had her pinned against the back wall leading to zone 4.

She just kept looking forward and didn't respond to anything I had just said. I was so mad, but I could not do anything to jeopardize my undercover status. So I simply left her standing right there. I'd deal with this stank hoe later.

I spent the rest of my shift in my assigned zone, ignoring everyone and everything.

Mikeela

Seeing my mother in that state had totally fucked up my vibe. I mean, I loved her, but her actions had left her children to fend for themselves at a very young age. My mother and her choices had left me questioning if I ever wanted to have children. I mean, I was a success in my professional life, but emotionally, I was so far gone. I didn't know if I could ever return to normal. To make matters worse, I had no idea where my client was at that moment. He had suddenly gone MIA, and when that happened, he was usually involved in more criminal activities. I needed to speak with his ass, and he had up and gone missing.

Maybe I should go by his office or his house. Nahh, forget that.

The way Murder's temper was set up, I might have to cut his ass tonight 'cause I wasn't gonna take no more shit from anybody. I needed a stiff drink and a change of scenery.

I had decided to drive down the coast and stay at the Hotel Miranda, a little upscale hotel spot I had discovered back in my playa days. I called ahead to make my reservations and headed in that direction. Fuck this night, and when I got settled, I ain't answering no phone calls. I am officially MIA for a few days. Let that nigga wonder where the fuck I was for a minute.

Co-Co

I was feeling bummed 'cause my visit to the Millville prison had been a waste, but you can rest assure that I planned on returning to the joint to accomplish my agenda. In the meantime, I had finally decided to return to Club Body after a week of not showing or calling. Fuck ole man Davidson. I was back at work 'cause I needed to get this money. I made my way to Davidson's office to check in and pretend like shit was all good. I knocked on the door, and he said, "Come on."

I guess that meant I could enter. So, I did. He looked surprised to see me. "So you finally decided to come to work. It's about damn time! The rotation is still the same. Take your ass on and get ready," Davidson's nasty mouth ass had said.

I quickly left his office before I said the wrong shit and ended up fired instead of dancing. As I entered the dressing room, all eyes were on me. I was hoping I didn't have to whip nobody's ass tonight. In order to avoid a confrontation, I just ignored the stares and went to my station to get prepared to dance.

Out of the blue, I heard this one bitch named Sunnie say, "Damn, I guess if my mama was sucking the boss's dick, I could come to work whenever I wanted too and still stay in rotation."

I calmly stood to my feet, made my way to where Sunnie was standing and asked, "Do we have a problem?"

She didn't have all that mouth now that I was in her face.

"I'm waiting on an answer, you hating ass bitch!" I said to Sunnie. Silence was all I heard.

"That's what I thought," I said to the whole dressing room.

"Fuck you, Sunnie and yo homegirls too. Nobody needs to worry about Co-Co and what I choose to do!" I screamed at the top of my lungs.

I made my way back to my area and finished my preparations to get on stage. Fuck these hoes! Nobody was gonna make me miss my money tonight, and I meant that. I had already whipped Sunnie's ass once. I guess she needed to be reminded of my boxing game again. Hell, I had no problems showing these bitches if they really needed me to. But if they knew what I knew, they had better fall back and stay in their lanes. I had no problems — I mean no problems — with fucking a bitch up.

Black

I wanted to check in with my superior on my undercover assignment, so I called Sergeant Mack to give him an update about what I had encountered at the prison. The phone rang for what seemed like a million times. Finally, he answered.

"Hello," he said into the receiver.

"Hello, Sergeant, this is Agent 2211, and I wanted to give you some information about a correctional officer by the name of Bre Watkins.

From what I have seen, I believe that she may indeed be involved in the drug problem invading Millville State Prison. I have seen her interactions with inmates and one inmate in particular by the name of Beachie Sims, who just so happens to be one of Samuel McWalters business partners. I have also seen Watkins in compromising positions with Mr. McWalters himself. I know there were some reports of her being involved with this organization. Well, I have seen for myself her suspicious behavior. I can say, in my professional opinion, this female is certainly involved with this contraband being brought inside Millville prison," I said.

Sergeant Mack simply replied with "That's interesting."

After an awkward silence, I just finally ended the conversation by saying, "Okay, Sergeant Mack. Have a great day."

I was not sure what to make of the conversation with the sergeant. It was strange to me. Anyway, I needed to think on my game plan on how to approach Watkins and smoothen our little situation over, because I needed this broad to believe I was cool and on her team. I was thinking that maybe I could gain some information to put her ass away for a very long time. I knew that Watkins was a major player, but who else was in on the game? My curiosity was certainly piqued, and I needed answers for my own sanity.

Mikeela

My phone had been ringing continuously for twenty minutes. It was of course Murder, and I was ignoring his scandalous ass. Apparently, he was just hanging up when I didn't answer and hitting the Redial. For twenty long ass minutes, this nigga kept calling instead of just leaving a message. My nerves were shot, and this motherfucker and his case were becoming a burden on my life.

The phone finally stopped ringing, so I guessed he got the message. I had avoided him for the moment, but I knew that I couldn't avoid him forever. After all, he was my client, and I knew that if I did anything to jeopardize this case, Murder would take it personally. So since I liked living above ground, I needed to get my shit together.

The image of Sand White popped in my head, and it prompted me to return Murderville's call. On the third ring, Murder answered. "So why the fuck you been avoiding my calls? Need I remind you of who the fuck I am? Why must we continue to revisit this issue of you ignoring my attempts to contact you?" this man said all this without saying *hello*.

I was a little taken aback, but I replied, "I needed to get my head together, so I was doing just that. I'm back now. What was it that you needed? How can I be of service to the great Samuel McWalters?"

"Aight, bitch, don't get jazzy with me. I was calling to see if you heard about Sand White washing up on the shore," he said, his voice dripping with guilt.

"Yeah, I saw the flashing news report," I calmly stated.

"Has anyone called you concerning any investigations regarding Sand White's demise or why he would be found dead, washed ashore?" Murder asked, pretending to be genuinely concerned.

I knew this nigga was putting on an act. He was no more concerned about Mr. White or his family. I bravely asked, "Should I be concerned? Is there anything you need to tell me? Were you involved in that man's demise in any form or fashion? Hell, you already have charges a mile long! You really need to chill and stay under the radar."

Murder responded, "Not at all! I am good over here, baby, not a stain on me. But fuck all that! Can I hit that tonight or what?"

"No," I simply stated.

"Fuck you, then!" he said and ended the call. I was left thinking that I never should have bothered calling his ass in the first damn place. This nigga always managed to leave me in my feelings every single time. I had decided to hide away and chill at Hotel Miranda for a few days to get my mind right.

I poured me a glass of Merlot and looked out at the coast. This shit right here was so relaxing. I wasn't gonna think about my problems, my sisters, my mother, or Murder. At this point, fuck everybody.

Co-Co

I managed to perform my set and collect my money without smashing that bitch Sunnie's head in. I exited the stage and went into the dressing room to gather my belongings and leave. As I turned around, I was standing face-to-face with MD's ass. I was too afraid to speak, so I was just prepared to listen.

"Murderville wants to see you tonight, so I am here to take you to him," MD said.

"Why can't I just follow you in my car?" I nervously asked.

"No, because your ass is going to be blindfolded until we get to the designated location. Now finish getting your shit! The boss is waiting," he said with a smirk on his face.

I was just like, *Fuck it! Let's go and get this over with.* "Let's go, you slime ass nigga," I said and followed MD outside to a waiting limo. Once we were in the limo, this nigga handed me a blindfold and instructed me to put it on. He checked to make sure the blindfold was secure on my face and that I could not see out of it. I heard him knock on the window, and I assumed this was to signal the driver to start driving out.

We began moving, and MD started rubbing his nasty hands up and down my legs. He was telling me how fine I was and shit. Ole thirsty ass. I still was dressed in my stage uniform, so you can say that I was damn near naked. I then felt his hands trying to spread my legs apart. I had those legs locked, and I was fighting against his ass like my life depended on it. He moved over from where he was sitting to position himself right next to me.

This motherfucker started licking my ear and rubbing my vagina. I was trying so hard to fight being aroused, but the shit wasn't working. Luckily, the driver informed us that we had reached our destination. Thank God, 'cause this nigga's breath had my damn stomach sour. I must've said something out loud because all of a sudden, MD said, "Shut up, bitch, and get out the damn car!" He then took my hand and led me into where I assumed Murderville was waiting. It seemed as if I could hear my heart beating. It felt as if it was about to pound out of my chest. I feared what and who was waiting for me.

Black

I wasn't sure how to act about Sergeant Mack's aloofness, but I couldn't worry about that now. Murderville had seen me outside the prison in uniform, so he knew I was working there as a detention officer. However, no one in Millville, no one from the hood, knew I was a cop. My professional life, in that regard, was still somewhat of a mystery. Some knew I had a connection to law enforcement. They just didn't know the depths of my true involvement, and that was by my design. I needed to remain approachable to the ones on the right side of the law, to the hood niggas, and thugs. So, remaining private about being a cop allowed me to maintain my hood cred.

At this point, I was thinking that since Murderville already knew me, I should use that to my advantage. Yes, that was exactly what I was going to do. I would approach Watkins about putting me on to whatever she got going on in the prison. Once I had been allowed to gain access to the inside of the operation, I would be able to connect names and bring that shit to a halt once and for all. I was thinking I needed to infiltrate that bitch and bring it crashing to the ground.

Surely, if I was able to contribute to stopping a drug ring inside Millville State Prison, my captain and the mayor would be very appreciative and offer a bitch a damn promotion. Maybe I could even get some recognition. I was excited about my plan, and I couldn't wait to speak to Watkins's dirty ass to set my plan in motion.

Mikeela

I had been tucked away at my little hotel paradise, just relaxing and in chill mode. I had not answered one fucking phone call from Murderville. By his voice mail message, he was quite angry, but I didn't give two fucks about him or his feelings at this point. I knew I was playing a very dangerous game with an unstable man, but I didn't want to be bothered.

I had scheduled myself a massage in my room, and they were running late. I hated for things to not go as scheduled. I was picking up the phone to call the front desk when there was a knock on the door. "Damn, it's about time," I said as I walked to the hotel room door. As I opened the door, I was prepared to go off, but instead of a person, there was a beautiful bouquet of flowers with a card attached. I was shocked because to my knowledge, no one knew where I was. I nervously took the card out of its little envelope, and it read as follows:

Hello Kee-Kee,

I hope you are enjoying your mini vacation. Surprise! I always know the location of all my hoes.

XOXO,

Murder

I was stunned, and the card slipped from my hand like that in a scene from a damn movie. Was this nigga having me followed? I didn't know if I was scared or turned on. I just shook my head. My morals and integrity had really taken a nosedive since I had started fucking with Murder's ass. *Where the hell is this damn masseuse?* was what I was thinking when the loud knocking at the door brought me back to reality.

"I hope this ain't Murderville," I said as I made my way to the door. I opened the door very slowly. Thank God it was the hotel masseuse! At this moment, I was so relieved and I didn't give a damn about her being an hour late. I just wanted the stress rubbed out my body. *Lawd have mercy! Something has gotta give.*

Co-Co

MD removed my blindfold. Once my eyes focused, I noticed I was in a room that seemed to be an office of some sort. MD instructed me to hold tight and Murderville would be with me shortly. Now, mind you, I was still in the outfit that I performed in, so I was nearly naked and freezing cold.

Eventually, in walked Murderville. Damn, this man was so sexy, but I kept reminding myself that he was the enemy. "Well, Ms. Dime Diva, long time no see. I'm not sure if I should be offended by the fact that you have not kept in touch with me. I think we should get reacquainted before I handle the business of you being on the witness list for the prosecution," Murderville said to me.

"Okay," I said, somewhat nervously.

I was too frightened to say anything else. This nigga began to remove his suit pants then his shirt and tie. In a matter of minutes, he was standing before me butt-naked, and what he meant by reacquainted suddenly became clear. I cleared my throat and nervously began to speak.

"Umm . . . umm, so you had me brought here to have sex with you?"

"Shut up and get over here" was his reply.

"Bend that ass over," Murder then instructed. I did what I was told to do. After all, I felt that I didn't have a choice. My ass was up in the air, and Murder entered with the precision of a pro. I had tried to resist exhibiting any signs of pleasure, but my body began to betray me with each stroke that Murder landed. Before long, I joined in. Shit, it had been a minute since anyone had made love to me!

So if you can't beat them, join 'em.

This man was gorgeous, and the dick service was A1. It felt good, and when my time came to return the favor, I certainly did that. The smile on his face was reward enough for me.

Murder and I finished up our impromptu sex

session with us being exhausted but satisfied. He dressed, and so did I. I sat down on the sofa and waited for this man to deliver his instructions and ultimatum. "So, Co-Co, it was brought to my attention that you are on the witness list to testify for the enemy. I know you know the street code and oath that snitches get stitches. I also know that you know I am a god in these streets and that I always have an ear to the ground. I know people, and I know everything. I assume that you are a smart woman, and I also assume that you know the consequences of speaking about my business," Murder said.

I just sat there, too afraid to speak or look him directly in the eye. He still had an erection, so my eyes and mind decided to focus on that. Hell, honestly, I was game for round 2. Sad situation, but hell, it was the truth.

Black

I had come to work early, trying to catch Watkins before we started our shift. I wanted to run the idea of me being put on by her to see if she took the bait. She was not in the parking area, and by the start of shift, she still had not appeared. So I assumed she had called off from work and that part of my plan would have to wait.

For the first time in a while, I was assigned to the zone that Beachie was housed in. I decided to start small talk to see if he was as loose in the mouth tonight as word on the street said he was. Most niggas like Beachie usually talked way too much just to get attention.

He was involved in a card game with some more inmates, so I just shouted, "Hey, Beachie. When you free, come to the bars and holla at me."

"Aight, boss," Beachie replied. It was customary for inmates to call detention officers boss man or boss lady. I hated that shit, but oh well. About five minutes later, Beachie was at the bars.

"Hey boss. What's good with your sexy black ass?" he was saying, trying to holla and shit.

It was funny as hell to me when a motherfucker that was locked up tried to flirt like they really had a chance or was sexy in their orange prison uniforms. I just shook my head and said, "Aight, man, I didn't call you up here for that."

"What the hell you want then?" he shot back.

"I just want to know if you have some information about the contraband that seems to be finding its way into the prison and what Watkins have to do with it," I shot back.

"Aww, man, so you want me to snitch? I ain't no snitch, boss," he said, trying to convince me. I laughed and said, "That ain't what I hear, and it damn sure ain't the word on the streets of the 'Ville. Them niggas say yo ass snitching like a bitch," I told him.

"Well, if I did know something, what the hell are you gonna give me in exchange for my information?" he asked in a somewhat seductive voice.

I kinda chuckled slightly and replied, "Hell, commissary, honey buns, is all I got for that ass. I ain't got no pussy for sale like Watkins, so you can get that out of your mind."

"I knew that, 'cause you look like you like the same thing I like anyway, but I guarantee, one ride on this dick and you would change yo mind for sho," he said with an air of arrogance. Beachie had started to get on my damn nerves, so I ended the conversation and went on my break.

As I was heading to the break room, officer Dante came up and started talking about some nonsense. She said, "Hey, ain't Chanel Rye your sister?"

I had a smile on my face 'cause I knew this bitch already knew the answer to her own question. To humor her ass I said, "Yes, why? What's up?"

"Oh, nothing really. Just a few days ago, she came up to visitation to visit that inmate named Beachie, but I can't remember what his real name is. She couldn't get her visit because he was in isolation due to that altercation he was in," Dante said.

"Oh yeah?" was all I could manage to say.

I knew Dante's ugly ass was probably trying to be funny and fish for information so her gossiping ass could start some shit up in here. Ole dumb ass. I wondered if the bitch was gay, 'cause why the fuck was her name Dante? Ain't that a boy's name? Anyway, the bitch had succeeded because my interest was piqued. What the fuck was Co-Co into, or what was she trying to do? It seemed that with every twist and turn, my damn sisters were mixed up in this shit more than Murderville and his damn thugs. Guess what? My mind was made up. I didn't give a damn if I had to arrest my own damn family to clean up this prison facility and the streets of Millville. That's what I was going to do. At this point, my job required me to be loyal to justice and my damn self.

Mikeela

I was awakened from a deep, deep slumber by my ringing cell phone. "Uhh! What time is it?" I said out loud into my empty hotel room. By the time I rolled over to answer my phone, it had stopped ringing. Then the hotel room telephone started ringing. I ignored that and turned back over to try to go back to sleep. Just as I was comfortable, my cell phone began ringing again. I was irritated by this time, and I snatched my phone up and answered.

"What? Helllooo! Who is this? Hey, if you not gonna say nothing, don't be calling my damn phone, playing games!" I continued.

"Umm, hello Kee. It's me, your mother," the voice said. I didn't know how to respond. One, I was ashamed at how I had answered the phone, and two, I still owed my mother an apology for how I had acted the last time I saw her.

"Yes, mother," I managed to say.

"Umm, I am callin' to say that you girls need to be careful with dealing with Murderville. I'm on these streets, and they be talking. He's scum and can only love himself. Please be careful, chile," my mother said, and the phone went silent.

I didn't know what to make of this semi warning from my mother, but I did know that she knew what she was talking about. Frankly, this shit scared me even more than I already was. With my nerves shot to hell, I could not return to sleep, so I decided to get dressed and walk on the beach. I needed to find some peace, and hopefully, this walk on the beach would be what the doctor ordered. If only for a moment, peace was what I needed.

Co-Co

I had finally been allowed to leave by Murderville, but not before he warned me to keep my mouth shut about his business. I didn't know why he felt the need to try to come and check me. Hell, I really didn't have any insider knowledge about what Murderville and his goons did daily. I knew he had me setting niggas up and he would send in somebody to rob them. I knew he had me and some other young girls tricking on the street. I also knew he had tricked my mother as well. So I guess on another note, maybe I did have some shit to testify to regarding that nigga and his antics.

I was driven back to the club and let out in front of my car with a final warning from MD about the security and safety that my silence would buy. I intended to be silent until the time was right and my plan was in place. Once that moment came, I was definitely ready to shine the light on those hoe ass niggas for all the drama they had brought upon me and my family. My only regret would be that I wouldn't have access to the sex game of Murder, 'cause if one thing was for sure, it was that that dude right there knew how to slang that dick. I was sprung, had been since I was fourteen years old, but my survival and the life of my children came first and foremost.

The sound of my cell phone snapped me from my thoughts. "What the fuck does Black ass want this time of the damn morning? I don't have time for her condescending ass right now. Fuck, fuck it!" I said and answered the phone. "What?"

Black

I was contemplating the news that Dante had laid on me about my sister Co-Co visiting or trying to visit Beachie at the Millville prison. I wondered what her motive was, but I wasn't stupid. I knew Co- Co had something up her sleeve, 'cause that was her MO — always wanting something for nothing. Ole ratchet ass!

I made a mental note to contact both Mikeela and Co-Co so that I could schedule a meeting with those two bitches. I needed to see how involved they were with this Murderville situation before we all found our asses six feet under. My sisters and I had not been close over the last few years, but I didn't want any harm to come to them. I could not live with myself if it did. So a meeting was necessary to clear all this "he says, she says" shit up.

My shift had just ended, so I rushed to the car and dialed Co-Co's number. I preferred to talk to her first 'cause our relationship was shaky, but we still got along better than Mikeela and I did. After the phone had rung for what seemed like a long ass time, I heard Co-Co saying "Whattt?" into the damn phone.

"Damn," I said, "you hoodrats don't say hello anymore! Ole rude ass!"

"Look here, Black, it's too damn early in the morning for this bullshit and for me to be playing with yo ass. What is it that you want? I'm not in the mood," Co-Co replied in what seemed all in one breath.

"Ohh, okay, sister dear," I began, "you must have had a bad night at the Ms. Shake Yo Ass contest last night, but I will overlook your stank ass attitude. The reason I called is I need to see you at my house tomorrow at around 3:00 p.m., and no is not an option."

"Bitch, you ain't my mama! You can't be demanding me to be no place," Co-Co replied.

"Umm, no. I am not your mother, but in order to save your life, your ass will be at my house at the aforementioned time!" I yelled into the phone.

"Aight bitch," she said and hung the phone up in my face. I just shook my head and continued on my mission and proceeded to call Mikeela.

"Hello," a sleepy voice said into the phone receiver. "You asleep?" I said into the phone.

"It is seven thirty in the morning, bitch! You know I was asleep. What do you want, Black? I don't have time for your damn games!" Mikeela snapped back.

"Okay, okay. I need for you to meet me at my house at 3:00 p.m. tomorrow," I told her.

"Why?" was her response.

"I want to go over some issues I have with you, Co-Co, and that no good nigga Murder," I told Mikeela.

"Well, I have client-lawyer privilege," she said back at me.

"I know that, but I have a feeling that more than that is going on. So like I said, see ya at three," and I hung up on her dumb ass.

Mikeela Rye was my eldest sister. Yes, I loved her, but she sure knew how to get on my last fucking nerve.

Mikeela

I felt so relaxed after my little getaway up the coast. My mini vacation had allowed for me to clear my head and come to the conclusion that I was going to drop Murderville as a client. This situation had gotten out of hand, and I had no control over my client's actions or how he portrayed himself to the media.

While I was at the hotel, I had called my secretary, Mrs. Wallace, to have her draw up a letter informing Samuel McWalters, a.k.a. Murderville, of my decision. The letter was to be sent certified mail. Hell, I was done with his trifling ass! At least I hoped I was done. For one, it was hard to just turn off emotions and feelings for a nigga on the dime. Number 2, my period was late and my ass was nervous.

Now Black was setting up meetings and shit like she was the damn president or FBI. I didn't want to deal with my sisters and family issues right now. However, it might be beneficial for me to touch base and let them know my decision not to represent Murderville anymore just in case my ass went missing.

Lawd, I just hope I don't have to slap the shit out of one of these bitches before the meeting even starts. I'ma go to the little meeting, but I'ma for sure pray.

Co-Co

I was feeling some type of way about the phone call with my sister Black. I didn't feel like going to no damn meeting with her or   that high maintenance ass Mikeela Rye. After the night I had with Murderville's ass, I just wanted to go home and hide away in the comfort of my bed for days.

I had an uneasy feeling that shit was about to get real. My plan to talk with Beachie had not worked out, and now it seemed as if I was working on borrowed time. My head was pounding from stress. My vagina was sore from Murder pounding the hell out of it. My whole damn body hurt. When I finally made it home, my ass planned on showering and going to sleep this damn night off.

I hadn't made up my mind yet if I was going over to meet with Black and Mikeela tomorrow. You know, it might not be a bad idea after all since I couldn't get to Beachie. I knew that sooner or later; I would need somebody on my team. I would certainly need somebody to watch my back. Even though I didn't fully trust these bitches, they were family and better than rolling solo. I wasn't a fool, though. I knew I needed to keep one eye open 'cause in this particular type of game, everyone had a motive or an agenda. First and foremost, I would always remain loyal to myself.

Black

I awoke to what seemed like a cloud hanging over my damn head. Today, my sisters and I would get together and sort out some shit that was long overdue. I hoped we would remain civil and respectful of one another. We had not been in the same room with one another for a while, and I knew that at first, it would probably be awkward. Hopefully though, we could get over that and accomplish a goal of allegiance to one another until this Murderville shit was said and done.

Lawd, I hope I've done the right thing by inviting my sisters to my house for this meeting.

I was nervous as hell, and it was only eight in the damn morning. I still had approximately seven more hours to go. I had contemplated inviting my mother, Earlene, but I decided against that for two reasons. One, I didn't know where she was staying at the moment, and two, I really wanted to focus on getting us girls on the same page regarding loyalty and family. I just figured my mother's presence would only hinder progress and maintain the focus on how fucked up of a childhood we all had because of her. Let's just face the fact that all three of our asses still had mommy issues, but we were not going to address that shit today.

On another note, I had not spoken to Sergeant Mack in a while about my undercover operation. For some reason, he was MIA and possibly being reassigned. This was some shit I didn't understand either, but again, I couldn't worry about it 'cause I had other shit I was focusing on. So regarding my assignment at Millville State Prison, I was kinda going rogue. I just hoped I didn't run into any problems that I couldn't handle alone. I didn't think anyone there knew that I was undercover yet, and that was why it was important for me to get a plan in action and get my information and get the fuck out before the shit hit the fan. My first choice of business was to interrogate my sisters and see what the hell they knew. I could then formulate a plan of action. I decided to get out of my bed and go for a run to clear my head. I needed all senses on board later on today to deal with the Rye girls 'cause I knew they would arrive ready to do battle.

Mikeela

I woke up wanting to call Black's ass and tell

her I was not coming. I didn't feel like arguing with Co-Co's dumb, trifling ass today. I hadn't made the phone call 'cause I was also curious about what Black wanted with us. We had not been in the same room together for a hot minute, so I just assumed it had something to do with Murderville and his case. I knew Co-Co was a witness for the prosecution, but Black's ass was just a detention officer at the prison. So for the life of me, I couldn't figure out what she was so interested in. I knew Black was nosy, but damn!

I had a doctor's appointment this morning to go and confirm what I already felt my body was telling me. Yes, indeed, all the signs were there: feeling tired, sleeping all damn day, being hungry as hell, and of course, having morning sickness. I was just going to the doctor's appointment hoping against hope that I was mistaken and the doctor would say I was just stressed instead of pregnant. I could not believe I had allowed my emotions to get so out of hand. Now I was sitting here, about to have a baby with a nigga that was about to go to prison for the rest of his natural life.

I knew it was too late to cry over spilled milk. I needed to suck this shit up and put my big girl panties on. This too should pass, but fuck that! I'ma cry and boohoo on this shit first. Then I would figure out how I would deal with the situation I was currently in. I knew one thing for sure: this would be a secret I would carry to my grave. No one would ever know who the father of this child was. No one could ever know, especially Black and Co-Co. I'd figure out the lie about the baby's father when the time came. First things first.

Let me get to this doctor's appointment and quit delaying the inevitable. Murder is my baby daddy. Well, I be damned – FML.

Co-Co

As I sat in my room, getting mentally prepared to face Mikeela and Black for the first time in a long time, I began to cry. The tears flowed, and I could not stop them. I didn't have the energy to try. I, for the life of me, could not figure out why the fuck I was so emotional. I had endured a lot over my short life span, and the past few weeks had been pure hell. I was hurting and emotionally drained. My children had to be sent away for their protection and my sanity.

I had been subpoenaed to testify against a man that had no problem killing me if he woke up on the wrong side of the bed. To top that off, the motherfucker kidnapped me, sexed me, and then threatened my damn existence. Murder was out of control and a danger to all he deemed a threat.

Yes, I have a family, but we were not close.

Hell, I didn't even know if I could trust their ass. Now ain't that bout a bitch! I would go to Black's house, looking for a good outcome, but my protective wall would definitely be up and I wasn't taking no shit from any one of them. And ohhh, I hoped Earlene's crackhead ass was not going to be there. I just could not deal with her nonsense today.

I started to get ready for the meeting with great anticipation. I needed to get there and get this shit done and over so I could focus on my getaway. I had finally made the decision to leave Millville once and for all. Once this Murder debacle was over, I was gonna be gone with the wind. This city had taken all that I was willing to let it. It was time for a change, and as soon as possible, I would be chilling in safety with the loves of my life. My two children. I was determined to make sure that my future turned out better than my past. *Once you know better, you do better.*

Black

Well, the time had arrived, and my two sisters just pulled up. I crossed my fingers and hoped nobody would get their ass beaten. The doorbell rang. I said a little prayer and opened the door with butterflies in my stomach and a fake smile planted on my face. A bitch was nervous, but I could handle whatever came from this. Whether positive or negative, it was gonna be whatever it was gonna be.

I directed Mikeela and Co-Co into my den area because if these bitches got violent, there wasn't much that could be broken in that room. After everyone was settled, I offered drinks and appetizers, trying to break the ice. In true to life stank form with attitudes in tow, they both declined. Anyway, I ignored the blatant attitudes from both these bitches and got down to business.

"So, Mikeela," I began, "you fucking Murder, defending him, or both?" Let the games begin 'cause I was ready to play, and I didn't plan on taking any prisoners.

Mikeela

I had left the meeting with Black and Co-Co feeling a little optimistic about mending our relationships with one another. We had not agreed on everything, however, we did agree to be on the same page and share useful information about Murder. I informed them that I had decided to drop Murder as a client. Black seemed relieved when she heard that bit of information. Co-Co never said much of nothing, which kinda made me suspicious of the little stripper girl. All in all, things went well and we basically were in agreement with wanting Murder convicted and off the streets of Millville. Murder going to jail would solve a lot of problems for a lot of people, myself included.

I didn't tell my dear sisters that I was currently pregnant with Murderville's seed. One, it didn't seem like the proper time, considering everyone in the damn room hated his ass. Secondly, it was not their damn business, and I hadn't figured out what exactly I was gonna do at this point about this baby. My cell phone began ringing, and I feared looking to see who was calling. Sure enough, Murder's name appeared. Damn, I didn't know what to do.

"Fuck it," I said and just answered the call.

"Hello," I said nervously into the phone.

"Hey, bitch, how you gonna inform me by certified mail that you done with my case? That's how you doing a nigga now? So you mad? You ain't got no love for me no more? That's cool 'cause I'm still in the family way. Check your message box. I just sent you a video. The starring roles belong to yours truly and someone close to you. Be easy," Murder said. He said all this without me getting anything in edgewise and hung up the damn phone.

I had a message on my phone from Murder,

but I was scared to look at it. I took a deep breath and clicked on the message and found that it wasn't a message but a video. I proceeded to click on the video to play it. Lo and behold, it was a video of Murderville fucking my sister Co-Co and of Co-Co giving him head service. My dear, sweet sister seemed to be in ecstasy. The look of pleasure on her face seemed familiar. I was sure I had those same looks when Murder was with me. The nigga definitely knew how to slang that pipe. I was hit with a flood of emotions. I was hurt, confused, and angry all at once. This video has definitely changed the game. Fuck an alliance with my sisters! I was going to be loyal to myself, and Co-Co the stripper would pay for sleeping with my man.

Co-Co

I left Black's house content for the moment. Yet I still had an uneasy feeling that shit was not all good. I decided to go get my finances in order and arrange for my belongings to be put in storage. I wanted everything done and in order just in case I needed to make a quicker exit than I had anticipated.

At the meeting at Black's place, I could feel the tension between Mikeela and me in the air. I didn't understand what personal issues she had with me. Maybe one day we could work it out. I knew she took issue with the fact that I chose to strip for a living, but hell, I took issue with her stuck-up ass attitude. She had abandoned us because we didn't fit into her lawyer high-class lifestyle. Guess what, though? The bitch was still from the same projects that I came from, and we both shared the same crackhead for a mother. She couldn't run from that.

Well, I had put into action things that I needed done in order for me to leave town. In a couple of days, I would leave the Millville projects for good. I had decided to stay the remainder of my days in Millville in a hotel room. I was prepared to jump from hotel to hotel if needed be. I couldn't leave Millville just yet because I still had to testify in this damn case the State was pursuing against Murderville and his goon organization. I didn't know how long it would take for it to come up on the docket, but my ass was antsy. I was wishing it would happen so I could experience some peace of mind and go and be with my children.

At this point, I didn't trust anyone, and I was living in a state of paranoia. It wasn't drug induced, but I was sure a quick high would certainly take the edge off. I didn't want to go down that road again. Plus seeing my mother succumb to the woes of drugs and leave her children behind had served as an ugly reminder of the cost of being an addict.

Mikeela and I hadn't really had a friendly exchange at Black's house earlier, so I was wondering why the fuck she was calling me now. I contemplated answering the phone 'cause I had seen enough of her ass for one day. But on the third ring and hoping for the best, I answered, "Hello."

"Co-Co?" Mikeela said.

"Who the fuck else is it gonna be? You called my number, right?" I replied.

"Ha-ha, okay, Co-Co, I was just checking. Hey, can you meet me at the little clubhouse out behind Club Body?" Mikeela said.

"Why?" I asked her curiously.

"I want to go over some stuff that I didn't really want Black in on," she simply stated.

"Umm, what time Kee?" I said.

"Well, tomorrow after you get off from the club, like around 1:00 a.m. or 2:00 a.m., would be fine," Mikeela replied.

"Damn, why so late? And why behind the club and not inside Club Body?" I asked Mikeela.

"The clubhouse behind provides us with more

privacy. You coming or not, bitch?" Mikeela said with venom in her voice.

"Bet," I said and disconnected the call. I was highly suspicious of this sudden knowledge and shit that Mikeela had to run by me. She was my sister, so surely, she didn't have any sneaky underhanded shenanigans up her sleeve. Maybe I would show up, maybe I wouldn't. I hadn't decided yet, but right now, I was taking my ass to bed. I was exhausted mentally, physically, and emotionally. Maybe, just maybe, I could find some peace in my dreams.

Black

I felt pretty good about the meeting with my sisters. I mean, nobody tried to kill anybody. I received the great news that Mikeela had finally come to her senses and dropped Murder as a client. I knew that dropping Murder as a client wasn't going to be so easy. I just hoped Kee knew this, and I hoped she was ready for the consequences of those actions.

Now that my sisters' and I were semi on the same page, I could focus on Watkins and what was going on in the state prison. I had yet to gather information from Beachie, but maybe I could speak to the inmate White Boy to see what he knew. I prepared to head to work, and hopefully, White Boy was in a talking mood 'cause I damn sure was ready to listen.

When I finally made it to work, everyone was all in an uproar. I passed by several different groups of people standing around, gossiping about some new inmate just booked in and housed in the prison. My curiosity was piqued, and I wanted to know who the hell everyone was so excited about. I didn't have long to wait to find out what I wanted to know.

The sergeant on duty that night got up to the podium to begin briefing by first conducting roll and then giving zone assignments. After that, he made a small speech, in which he informed us that Samuel McWalters had been booked into the Millville State Prison within the last hour. Sergeant was saying some other stuff along with that, but the moment I heard that nigga's name, I zoned the fuck out.

Murderville was in Millville State Prison now! Ain't that some shit? I wondered if I could keep his ass locked up for good. I wasn't sure if I could, but I was damn sure gonna try.

Mikeela

So I came to find out Murder was calling me as he was being arrested on suspicion of murder.

The victim was none other than Sand White. I can tell you I was not surprised. I wasn't sure if this charge was gonna be added to the shitload of other charges he was already facing or if this was going to be a whole separate case altogether. I was sure they must have some type of evidence to go ahead and arrest him on this charge. I could feel a headache coming on. Regardless of what I had said before, I was still in love with Murder, and yes, I was still gonna be loyal to this nigga until the day I died.

I had received a call from MD telling me that I was to meet with Murder at the prison tomorrow to go over some case-related details. When I proceeded to inform MD that I was no longer the attorney on the case, he was not trying to hear it. MD said Murder didn't take no for an answer and, if I loved living and breathing, I would be at the prison to discuss case matters with him. So since I did indeed like living and breathing, I agreed to be at Millville State Prison to handle my business. Damn!

Co-Co

I decided to meet Kee-Kee after my set tomorrow night around 1:00 a.m. in the clubhouse. I, for the life of me, could not figure out what the hell she had to tell me, but if the bitch wanted a fight, I was ready for that showdown as well. I managed to get through my set. It wasn't my best show, but I still got money. These niggas weren't interested in good. Hell, they were interested in naked ass. So living up to those standards was easy as hell. I gathered my money from the stage and made my way back to the dressing room to prepare my mind to meet with Mikeela tomorrow night. Lawd, please don't let me have to whip her ass, 'cause the way I was feeling, Mikeela might not walk away from this confrontation alive. I gathered my belongings and prepared to go home. I was ready to get some rest.

Black

I couldn't believe that Murder was actually being housed in Millville State. I had figured that he was Mr. Untouchable, what with all the shit he had managed to get away with over the years. He also had some high-profile people on his payroll, so like I said before, I was very surprised that the law went and arrested his ass. I was excited but still surprised.

After settling into my assigned zone, I walked around to the isolation zone, where the high-profile inmates were kept away from the normal population. I just wanted to make eye contact with this nigga. I wanted to see with my own eyes. I didn't know how long he would be there. However, I was gonna relish in the fact that justice was sweet. Even though it might be just for a moment, I was still gonna enjoy seeing Murder behind bars, where his ass belonged.

Upon my entering the isolation zone, I saw Officer Watkins, and I immediately rolled my eyes. I should have known this whore would be in the zone that was housing her boss and her man, both of whom went by the name Murder, a.k.a. Samuel McWalters, so I walked up on Watkins.

"Hey," I said, "is it true? Is the great Murderville finally in isolation lockup?" Watkins seemed angered by my question.

"Yes bitch, he is," she replied. "He's over there! Hell, he can talk and hear you. Go over to him and get all your damn questions answered."

Watkins had continued being a smart-ass. I looked over in the direction of the single cells, and indeed, Murder was standing in the cell window, motioning for me to come over. Reluctantly I went. "What's up, Murder?" I asked.

"Shit ain't nothing but the rent, and your price just went up," he replied to me. I kinda giggled, a bit confused at his response.

"What that mean?" I asked him.

"It means that you need to tell your bitch ass sisters, Mikeela and Co-Co, to watch out. I know everything that happens in Millville. I know names and addresses, so you bitches best understand that my reach is long. If I don't get what I want, everyone is gonna suffer. Mikeela is still under my spell regardless of whether she is my lawyer or not. Co-Co has always been my whore and always will be, and your mother is addicted to my crack pipes. So if you and those bitches want to stay among the land of the living, you will remain loyal to me," Murder said in a long rant.

"Loyal to you? Nigga, please," I responded while turning to walk away.

Evidently, this nigga was tripping, and I had heard all the bullshit I wanted to hear from his ass tonight. The speech Murder had given had rattled my feathers a little. I wondered how the hell my family was so involved with this man and his organization. Something had to give. The time to pay the piper was near. I was left wondering who in the hell would be left standing. Who was strong enough to survive?

Mikeela

I was not able to sleep at all last night. I tossed and turned all damn night. My mind was occupied with my scheduled visit with Murder in

Millville State. Hell, I had properly relieved myself as his counsel, but this motherfucker had refused to take no for an answer. I reluctantly rolled out my California king and went into the bathroom to prepare for a showdown with the great Murderville. Of course, I dressed to impress and get his attention, but I was still a nervous wreck.

As I passed through security, I recited some words of encouragement to myself to calm my nerves. I was led into the conference room, where clients could meet with their counsel. I paced the room back and forth. I was too nervous to sit and wait for officers to bring Murder in the room. I knew that officers would be in the room with me, but shit, I was still scared as hell to be so close to this nigga. I managed to gain some type of control over my nerves, and as soon as I did, officers were ushering Murder's ass into the room. I sat down, trying to act as brave and professional as possible.

"Hello, beautiful," Murder said, greeting me.

"Good morning, Mr. McWalters," I replied. I was trying to keep this shit strictly business.

"Ohh, it's like that," he said, sounding somewhat irritated.

"I am kinda at a loss for why you wanted to meet with me since you are no longer my client."

I said to him.

"Well now, Ms. Rye, you know it will never be that easy," Murder said, and the moment I heard him speak those words, my blood ran cold and I began to shake uncontrollably.

Murder noticed me shaking and tried to reach out and touch my hands. However, I was able to move them from his reach just in time.

"Well then, Ms. Rye, I see how things have turned," Murder began, but I didn't reply. "Did you receive the little video I sent you?"

"Co-Co can sure ride like a pro, don't you think?" Irritated, I slammed my fist on the table and said, "What the fuck do you want with me? Why am I here?"

Murder cleared his throat, laughed, and said, "I called you here because I wanted to see your face and to inform you of the fact that you will never really be free from me. I will see you soon on the other side of these bars. You will pay for abandoning me and being disloyal."

With that last statement, this nigga motioned to let the officers in the room know that he was ready to leave and that our interview was over. I didn't know what to make of this little exchange between the two of us. I just wanted to go home and start putting my life back in the state it was in before I accepted Samuel McWalters as a client.

I decided to try to call Co-Co to cancel our meeting for tonight. I didn't feel like getting into an altercation with her ass tonight. At this point, I didn't want to be around anyone. I dialed Co-Co's number, and the phone began to ring. *Shittt!* She didn't pick up the phone call, so I just hung up without leaving a message. Hell, I figured she would call me back or get the message once she saw that I didn't show up at the scheduled time.

The visit with Murder had me emotionally exhausted. I just immediately returned to my home and headed to the bedroom to sleep this shit off. The meeting with Murder had not accomplished anything pertaining to business or his case. It was just a ploy for him to fuck with my emotions and get in my head. To tell you the truth, the motherfucker had succeeded at both.

Co-Co

I saw Kee-Kee's name appear on my phone, but I ignored the call. I didn't want to deal with her ass just yet. We had already planned to meet later on after my shift tonight. Being in my sister's presence later on tonight would probably be all of her I could take for a minute. I had no idea why Kee wanted to meet, but I was sure it had some drama attached to it. I was sure it also had something to do with Murder's dirty ass.

At our little meeting at Black's house, Kee claimed she was done with him, but I knew that was some bullshit. Mikeela loved Murder's dirty drawers, and she could save that song and dance for some other sucker. That nigga had done so much shit to our family, and she still was gonna defend his no good ass in a court of law. Where the fuck was her loyalty? Regardless of whether we talked or not, we were family tied together by blood.

Fuck a nigga! Fuck the bullshit! Blood is supposed to be thicker than water. Yeah, tonight I would be giving my high-class ass sister a piece of my mind. Tonight, this bitch would be put in her place and given a lesson by me on what it meant to be loyal. If I needed to smash that ass to get my point across, I would be more than happy to do that shit as well. Yes, indeed, I was looking forward to this meeting with sister dear tonight. Bring it on!

Black

So after my conversation with Murderville, in which he kinda threatened me and my family, I didn't really know how I should feel. I knew that he meant exactly what he said, but I didn't know what my first move should be. I had called both

Mikeela and Co-Co, but neither of them answered the damn phone. I had no idea where my mother was, so trying to reach her was a lost cause. I wanted to at least let my sisters know what had developed so that they could at least be aware of the situation and take precautions to protect themselves.

As soon as I made it home, I tried calling my sergeant to let him know about the threat that Murderville had seemingly made on my life, but this motherfucker had somehow disappeared or was just ignoring my calls. Sergeant Mack had been acting strange. I needed to know where he was. Hell, my life and the lives of my family members were at stake. My mind and instincts were telling me to fuck the system and just go rouge. I knew that if I was backed into a corner, the project survival system in me was gonna come out.

I refused to be a victim and get caught slipping. My ass had some shit up my sleeve as well. I picked up my phone and dialed Co-Co's number. The shit went straight to voicemail. I dialed Mikeela's number — the same shit. *Fuck, where are these bitches!* I need to talk to them ASAP.

Mikeela

My phone was getting on my damn

nerves. First, MD, and then Black. Hell, it seemed like they were tag-teaming and taking turns calling my ass. I was ignoring all calls at this time. Eventually, I just powered my phone off. I was done with drama, at least for tonight. My life had really gotten off course as of late, and I had no clue how to fix it.

Murderville was in jail, not dead, so that meant he could still do whatever the hell he wanted to do to whomever he chose to do it. That meant somebody's ass could still come up missing and fucked up. I had a feeling I was at the top of the list. This thought alone made my ass very nervous. I was feeling some type of way about changing my mind about meeting Co-Co and not being able to contact her on her cell phone. I knew she would be pissed off, but eventually, the bitch would get over it. Hell, I didn't care. Well, yeah, I kinda did, but in the big scheme of things, Co-Co couldn't stay mad forever. Mad Dawg had been continuously calling me since I left the meeting with Murder earlier today. I was stressed out after meeting that nigga in the conference room of Millville State Prison. I felt so exhausted mentally, physically, and emotionally. I just wanted to go home and sleep this shit off — maybe. At least I was praying to wake up in the morning with a clear head and better attitude. But before I headed to bed, I tried Co-Co's cell one last time. This time it went straight to voicemail.

Defeated, I made my way to my room, hoping for a peaceful night's sleep. At this point, I was thinking, *Two tears in a bucket, so fuck it.* My peace of mind was the only thing that I was concerned with at that moment. I wanted to crawl in my bed and sleep this day off, and that was exactly what I did.

Co-Co

I was excited about meeting Mikeela tonight. Finally, we would be able to work out our differences, and if that meant fighting the shit out, then oh well, it was whatever on my end. I stayed ready for family, friend, or foe. This meeting right here had been a long time coming. The bitch better not cancel either. I needed to put thoughts of Kee-Kee and the meeting on the back burner for the moment. I gotta get my mind on my money, so I'ma let that subject chill.

As I went in the club tonight, it was pretty full and jumping for a weeknight. I guessed these niggas got their girls' income tax checks or something. I didn't care where the money came from 'cause if they were throwing it and it folded, I was for damn sure gonna take it. Let it rain in this motherfucker tonight. I gotta get this paper. It was about time for me to hit the stage. As I made my way to the front, I was hit with an eerie feeling. Like something wasn't right. My instincts were trying to tell me something, but what? Anyway, I had to push that shit out of my head. I had never been nervous to perform on stage or shake my ass, so that wasn't it. I loved stripping, I loved the money, and I damn sure loved the attention. So I didn't know what was up with this feeling, but I did know that it wasn't gonna stand in the way of my coins.

I refocused and approached the stage like the champ I was and gave the crowd of thirsty-ass niggas the show they were looking to see from Co-Co "the Dime Diva" Rye.

Black

I still hadn't come to grips with, nor did I know how to react to, the semi threat that I received from Murder. I must admit that I was definitely in my tinder about it. I knew who he was in the streets, and I also knew that if he said it, he meant it. The streets had christened him Murder 'cause if you crossed him, that was exactly what you'd get: murdered. I still could not contact my supervisor, Sergeant Mack, to save my life. He had gone MIA in the middle of a fucking investigation that he was supposed to be in charge of. There was something weird about that shit. I needed to get myself situated to survive whatever was about to come my way. I knew that Watkins was dirty. Beachie was dirty and working on the same team. Well, hell, Beachie was playing for both teams. I never got close or questioned him, but at this point, talking with him wouldn't make a difference. The situation was well beyond that.

My cell phone rang, interrupting my thoughts. When I looked at the name occupied by the number, I knew shit just got real. It was MD, Murder's right-hand man. What the fuck did he want, and how in the hell did this motherfucker get my damn number? Needless to say, I didn't answer the call. I wasn't ready to enter that realm of problems just yet. I knew that soon I would have to have that conversation, because I couldn't run or hide forever.

Kee-Kee

I was definitely thanking the Good Lord for a good night's sleep. My peace of mind and my soul needed that rest. I looked at my cell phone and saw that I had ten missed calls from Co-Co. What the hell did she want? And what the fuck was so important that she had called me so many damn times? I knew she would be upset 'cause I didn't meet her as planned, but damn. Anyway, I'd deal with that later.

I had decided to go on an extended vacation. I was going to close my practice for a while, regroup, and come back refreshed, stronger than ever. I had phone calls to make in order to get my affairs in order. I wanted to take care of my staff by finding them alternative offices to work in until I made my return. Due to my great financial planning, I could afford to offer them a severance package to hold them over as well. I had called my secretary, Mrs. Wallace, so she could arrange for an office meeting later on today to inform them of my decision. I had allowed for a man to derail my focus and dictate how I performed in my profession. I knew that I most certainly needed to detoxify this man from my mind. The problem though was that I didn't know if I could remove him from my heart and soul. Honestly, I loved this man. I had loved him since my childhood days of growing up in the Hudson projects. I hadn't quite figured out what I would actually do or where I would actually go. I just knew I needed to be done in order for me to maintain my sanity and regain my integrity with my colleagues. But the very first thing on my agenda today was to visit my doctor.

I had been stressed out, and nobody had been responding accordingly. My doctor's appointment was at 1:00 p.m. today, so I decided to go back to sleep until noon. I was waiting until much later to deal with Co-Co and her drama. Ten missed calls. I shook my head and laid my head on my pillow. Soon I drifted back to sleep.

Co-Co

I had finished my set around 1:30 a.m. I was running late, but I didn't care, 'cause those niggas were making it rain in the club tonight and I needed my coins. I rushed off the stage, grabbed an overcoat out of the dressing room, and exited the side door of Club Body to get to the building behind it, ready to meet Kee-Kee. I was anxious to let her get whatever she seemed to have on her mind out in the open so she could stop with the bullshit once and for all. I entered the building, expecting her to be there, but she wasn't. Damn, I was thirty minutes late, though. Where was ole sister dear? I took a seat, pissed off and ready to give Kee-Kee the business as soon as she came through the door. I positioned my chair facing the door. I valued my time. I had shit to do too. Requesting a meeting and then not being on time was straight disrespectful. I guess I had dozed off because I awoke to a gun stuck to my temple. The person at the other end was MD, Murderville's bitch. I was scared shitless! I had a million things running through my head.

How the hell did this motherfucker know that I was here? Surely not. . . surely my own blood didn't set me up behind a no-good nigga like Murder! I immediately went into survival mode, looking around the room for a weapon and a means of escape.

"Well, well, Dime Diva, we meet again," MD said. "I surely do hate that it is under these dire circumstances. However, business is business," he continued. I guess he must've read my mind, 'cause he simply said, "Kee-Kee." I just shook my head in disbelief, and the tears started flowing nonstop. I knew that we were not close, but we were tied by blood. How in the world could my very own sister set me up and betray me for the second time? First, she left me to fend for myself in the projects when we were young, and now she led me to this situation to face this nigga, MD, alone. I guessed that blood being thicker than water didn't mean shit to Mikeela Rye, but I couldn't think about that now. I had to get out of this shit I was currently in. So I said, "MD, why it gotta be like this? You gonna kill me over some bullshit? What have I ever done to you?"

Black

I finally found out why I couldn't get in touch with my sergeant, who was in charge of my undercover assignment. The motherfucker had been fired and charged with taking bribes from the criminals he was supposed to be bringing to justice. I knew something was not right with his ass. How in the hell could you take an oath to protect the citizens of Millville and then betray them with the love of money?

I wondered if he was on Murderville's payroll as well. I thought so. That was why Sergeant Mack was not surprised by my briefing on Officer Watkins. He already knew because he was receiving his cut off the top. I wondered if the warden of Millville State Prison was also on the payroll. These people had no sense of ethics and morals. This new information just clarified for me that I needed to take my life and the life of those that I love in my hands. Sergeant Mack's dirty ass had put my life in danger. This meant that all that Murder knew was that I was working undercover all along, and that was why he was so comfortable with threatening me. I had been thinking, and I believed that Officer Watkins had no idea about my assignment. I just wanted to know why Murder never told her. My take on it was that Murder was just using that dumb bitch, and as soon as she served her purpose for him, he would discard her ass like the trash she was.

Since I believed that my undercover identity had been compromised, I decided that I would not be stepping foot back into Millville State. Those motherfuckers could send someone else to finish that assignment. Hell, I didn't give a fuck what happened; they didn't give a fuck about my life, so to hell with it! I did, however, need to finish this shit with Murderville and my family. I was still an officer of the law, and I took my oath seriously, but the loyalty that I had for my blood run deeper. So this girl from the hood would say that if push came to shove, it would forever be blood over bullshit all day, every day.

Mikeela

I made it to my doctor's appointment. I was informed that my blood pressure was high and that if I didn't take it easy, I would be on bed rest for the length of my pregnancy. That was some bullshit. I told my doctor that I had been under some extreme stress these past three weeks but that I had taken measures to relieve some of the stress. I also informed the doctor that I was taking leave from my job and leaving town. I was told that the baby was healthy and growing well. I was happy about that news. I knew this baby was not created in the most positive of circumstances, but I had grown to love the creation growing in my belly.

The bonding between mother and child had taken place, and I had decided to keep this child despite who the father was. I had not thought past giving birth, but my mind had been made up. This was my baby, and I would love it to the best of my ability. I, Mikeela Rye, was giving birth, and I was going to be a mother. I probably should go to therapy and get over my mommy issues before my due date. I probably should also mend my relationship with my sisters so that I could have as much help with this child as I could get.

It takes a village to raise a child, and I most definitely would need all the help I could get. All this kumbaya shit gotta wait a minute. In due time, hopefully, everything would work out for good. As of now, though, I needed to get my affairs in order so that I could skip town for a while. I had not decided where I wanted to go yet. I was thinking maybe a trip to the country would be good for my soul. Yes, that was exactly what I wanted to do, go to the country and renew my mind. Toco, Texas, would be my place of solace for a minute until I decided to return to my life and practice law in Millville.

Co-Co

MD responded, "Personally, Co-Co, I like you, and personally, I would like to sex you. I am not in control. The boss has delivered an order, and I have no choice but to obey."

"So like a bitch, you just gonna kill someone on some bullshit type of situation?" I replied.

He simply stated, "It's my job."

He was looking at me with that look that men got when they wanted to fuck. I knew that look well, and at this point, it was welcomed 'cause maybe by using sex, I could save my life. I knew one damn thing; if I made it out alive, Mikeela's ass had better take cover 'cause this setup right here most definitely meant that all truces were off. I had earned the right to declare war on that bitch, and you can bet your last dollar that vengeance would be mine. That bitch's ass was grass. All of a sudden, there was a loud commotion in the rear of the room toward the door. MD and I exchanged glances for a brief moment and looked in the direction of the noise. Standing there with two armed goons, who were dressed in black, was my mother. To say I was shocked and relieved all at the same damn time would be an understatement.

My mother said, "Hey motherfucker! What are you trying to do to my child? Co-Co, pull your damn clothes up and get the hell out of here *now*! Go, go!" My mother was screaming at me to go.

"But," I began.

"But what?" my mother said, cutting me off mid-sentence. "Get your shit together and go!" I didn't know how to respond, so I just composed myself as best as I could and left the building. As I set foot outside, I heard a barrage of shots. I took off like a lightning bolt, heading toward my car. I didn't look back, not once, for fear of what I would see.

I was too afraid to go home, so I went to a hotel until daylight and got my thoughts together. I was about to strike to even the score and get the hell out of dodge. As soon as the sun came up, my ass was heading to do my dirt and get the fuck out of town. Fuck this shit! If the prosecution and the city of Millville wanted me to testify against Murderville, they would have to find my ass, but my sister Kee-Kee, now that was another story. That bitch better hope I didn't find her, 'cause her ass would feel my wrath. I was hurt, but I couldn't deal with those emotions just yet. I had to keep my mind focused on the mission.

How the hell are you gonna set up your own sister, your own blood, for the love of a nigga?

Oh yes indeed, vengeance would be mine, and karma would most definitely be a bitch that paid my dear sister a visit. What was a person to do when betrayed by blood? The only thing I knew was to get even. It might not be right, but shit sure would be even.

Black

I had decided to drive by Co-Co's job — hell, if stripping is a job — to catch up and see if everything was copacetic. As I pulled up in the parking lot, there were police officers, crime scene investigators, and onlookers all over the damn place, making it hard to find a place to park, so I could find out what the hell was going on.

After eventually finding a place to park, I got out of my vehicle to see what the hell had happened and if it involved my damn sister Co-Co. At the onset, I was not alarmed because crazy shit was also happening at the other establishments owned by Davidson's ole ass. Club Body was not any different. I recognized one of the officers from my unit, so I approached to get the 411 on the disturbance and what the fuck was going on. The officer I had approached was named Gary Willis.

"Hey, Willis, what's going on here now?"

"They found a body in the building behind the club. I think his street name was MD, the enforcer for Murderville," Officer Williams said. The moment I heard the name MD, my blood ran cold, because this motherfucker had just called my phone a few hours ago. I hoped he didn't have his damn phone on him when his ass got shot. If he did and they did a proper investigation, I would have to answer why the hell he called me hours before he was murdered. I also hoped that Co-Co's ass didn't have anything to do with this shit, but I had a sinking feeling in the pit of my stomach that was telling me that she was indeed involved.

I hurried my ass to my car and left the fucking scene. If they wanted to question me, they were gonna have to find me. I immediately began calling Co-Co's cell, but it would go straight to voicemail. What the fuck was going on? No one was answering their damn phones, and the shit was pissing me off! I could not deal with this. Shit was getting out of control.

Co-Co and Mikeela

I had swooped by Mikeela's house and convinced her to go for a drive. I was driving erratically.

"Co-Co, slow this damn car down! What the fuck is wrong with you?" Mikeela screamed. I was in a zone, and what she was saying to me seemed like nonsense. I eventually made it to an undisclosed location just outside the city limits of Millville. Of course, the bitch didn't want to get out of the car.

"Why are we at this dump, Co-Co? What the fuck is going on? Why are you acting so fucking crazy, bitch? Take me home now!" Mikeela said. I pulled my gat out and pointed it at her head. I went close and positioned myself so I could whisper in her ear. "Sister dear, payback's a bitch, and it's time to pay the piper. You had one choice to make, and you chose that nigga Murder. Well, there are consequences to all choices, and I gotta make it even. My whole life you decided to disrespect your family, you disloyal bitch!" I said.

"But, Co-Co, why are you doing this? We are sisters, we're family," Mikeela said.

"Yes, indeed, we are. We were also family when you set me up to meet MD instead of you so that he could kill my ass," I replied.

"I don't know what you are talking about!" Mikeela said through her tears. I proceeded to slap the shit out of her. She was pissing me off standing in my face, lying about setting my ass up. I was having mixed emotions. I loved my sister, but my upbringing and survival mentality could not let this type of betrayal go.

I pulled my black stocking cap over my face, pointed my weapon, and aimed at Mikeela. With tears streaming down my face, I recited, "Loyalty, sisterhood, and respect." These were the words my sisters and I would recite in our childhood days to signify our bond. I didn't know where shit went wrong, but these were the cards I had been dealt. Again, my emotions were getting in the way. I refocused, steadying my aim. Fuck it! I pulled the trigger. Mikeela let out the most agonizing scream. "I'm pregnant!" Mikeela screamed. I fired again and again. At this point, I had zoned out. I simply turned and exited the building. I sprinted to my rental and headed toward the expressway to get the hell out of dodge and leave all this shit behind. I thought I had heard Mikeela scream that she was pregnant.

I hoped to God that I was hearing things. Oh well, the shit was done. Fuck this city, fuck my family. Loyalty didn't mean shit, not even to blood.

Get connected with Author Anitra Ferguson on social media

 writingqueen

 anitrawrites

Anitra Ferguson

www.ingramcontent.com/pod-product-compliance
Lightning Source LLC
Chambersburg PA
CBHW021336190726
48288CB00003B/1134